DESTINY OF LOVE

SEAL Brotherhood: Legacy Series

Book 6

SHARON HAMILTON

SHARON HAMILTON'S BOOK LIST

SEAL BROTHERHOOD BOOKS

SEAL BROTHERHOOD SERIES

Accidental SEAL Book 1

Fallen SEAL Legacy Book 2

SEAL Under Covers Book 3

SEAL The Deal Book 4

Cruisin' For A SEAL Book 5

SEAL My Destiny Book 6

SEAL of My Heart Book 7

Fredo's Dream Book 8

SEAL My Love Book 9

SEAL Encounter Prequel to Book 1

SEAL Endeavor Prequel to Book 2

Ultimate SEAL Collection Vol. 1 Books 1-4 /2 Prequels

Ultimate SEAL Collection Vol. 2 Books 5-7

SEAL BROTHERHOOD LEGACY SERIES

Watery Grave Book 1

Honor The Fallen Book 2

Grave Injustice Book 3

Deal With The Devil Book 4

Cruisin' For Love Book 5

Destiny of Love Book 6

Heart of Gold Book 7

BAD BOYS OF SEAL TEAM 3 SERIES

SEAL's Promise Book 1

SEAL My Home Book 2

SEAL's Code Book 3

Big Bad Boys Bundle Books 1-3

BAND OF BACHELORS SERIES

Lucas Book 1

Alex Book 2

Jake Book 3

Jake 2 Book 4

Big Band of Bachelors Bundle

BONE FROG BROTHERHOOD SERIES

New Year's SEAL Dream Book 1

SEALed At The Altar Book 2

SEALed Forever Book 3

SEAL's Rescue Book 4

SEALed Protection Book 5

Bone Frog Brotherhood Superbundle

BONE FROG BACHELOR SERIES

Bone Frog Bachelor Book 0.5

Unleashed Book 1

Restored Book 2

Revenge Book 3

Legacy Book 4

Paradise: In Search of Love
Love Me Tender, Love You Hard

NOVELLAS
SEAL You In My Dreams Magnolias and Moonshine

PARANORMALS

GOLDEN VAMPIRES OF TUSCANY SERIES
Honeymoon Bite Book 1
Mortal Bite Book 2
Christmas Bite Book 3
Midnight Bite Book 4

THE GUARDIANS
Heavenly Lover Book 1
Underworld Lover Book 2
Underworld Queen Book 3
Redemption Book 4

FALL FROM GRACE SERIES
Gideon: Heavenly Fall

SUNSET BEACH SERIES
I'll Always Love You

NOVELLAS
SEAL Of Time Trident Legacy

All of Sharon's books are available on Audible,
narrated by the talented J.D. Hart.

ABOUT THE BOOK

The heart has no limits. Love grows from tragedy.

Luke and Julie adopt his sister's and her brother's three children after their parents are killed in a traffic accident. Suddenly, their finances take center stage as they embrace their new blended family just at the point where Luke had been planning to leave the Teams and Julie was in line for a big promotion.

But being a man of action with a somewhat fragile ego, will assuming the role of stay-at-home dad, changing diapers and wearing an apron fill the billet while Julie becomes the sole breadwinner?

And what happens when an investigation into the car accident reveals perhaps it wasn't? As danger lurks all around them, Luke discovers his new unexpected role of family protector is one he's been rehearsing for a decade.

And he was made for this!

AUTHOR'S NOTE

I always dedicate my SEAL Brotherhood books to the brave men and women who defend our shores and keep us safe. Without their sacrifice and that of their families—because a warrior's fight always includes his or her family—I wouldn't have the freedom and opportunity to make a living writing these stories. They sometimes pay the ultimate price so we can debate, argue, go have coffee with friends, raise our children, and see them have children of their own.

One of my favorite tributes to warriors resides on many memorials, including one I saw honoring the fallen of WWII on an island in the Pacific:

> "When you go home
> Tell them of us, and say
> For your tomorrow,
> We gave our today."

These are my stories created out of my own imagination. Anything that is inaccurately portrayed is either my mistake or done intentionally to disguise something I might have overheard over a beer or in the corner of one of the hangouts along the Coronado Strand.

I support two main charities. Navy SEAL/UDT Museum operates in Ft. Pierce, Florida. Please learn about this wonderful museum, all run by active and former SEALs and their friends and families, and who rely on public support, not that of the U.S. Government. www.navysealmuseum.org

I also support Wounded Warriors, who tirelessly bring together the warrior as well as the family members who are just learning to deal with their soldier's condition and have nowhere to turn. It is a long path to becoming well, but I've seen first-hand what this organization does for its warriors and the families who love them. Please give what your heart tells you is right. If you cannot give, volunteer at one of the many service centers all over the United States. Get involved. Do something meaningful for someone who gave so much of themselves, to families who have paid the price for your freedom. You'll find a family there unlike any other on the planet. www.woundedwarriorproject.org

CHAPTER 1

"**H**EY, SON, IS Julie home?" Mr. Christensen's voice was softer than usual. Luke was barely able to hear his father-in-law.

"No, she's still down at the school. It's parent-teacher night tonight. What's up?" he asked.

At first, there was silence. Julie's dad was normally very talkative, quite chatty, and always upbeat. Luke's antennae began to pick up something dark and ominous.

An involuntary sigh preceded the older man's gradual high-pitched whine followed by a collapse of his voice altogether. He started to sob into the phone. Luke plugged his right ear so he could make out the mumbling words. "I-I don't know how to say this."

"What is it? Is something wrong with Melinda?"

"No, not Melinda. It's Colin and Stephanie."

Luke and Julie's two girls were playing in the back-yard in their new blow-up pool they'd bought the day before. September could be warm in San Diego, and the new pool gave them comfort, as well as occupied them for hours. The happy splashing and screaming, like two young sisters who competed in everything, sounded normal. But Luke knew this was not a normal call, nor a normal day. If Julie's dad's call was just a hello to touch base, Luke would've been out the back door screaming at them to be quiet so he could listen. But with Mr. Christensen in his current state, Luke dared not do that, and he halfway didn't want to even hear him.

Oh, shit. Here it comes.

"I'm sitting down, Dad. Tell me what it is." He steeled himself for news he knew was going to be horrible.

"Stephanie and Colin were at that convention in Las Vegas, and on their way back—they were almost home…" He broke down again.

"Take your time. Breathe, Dad."

"We've been having a marvelous time watching the kids for them. They've been little angels, bless their hearts." His voice hitched again, and he began to tear up.

It was hard for Luke to listen to his struggle. He wished he was there to comfort him.

"They needed this getaway so badly. They've been working so hard."

"Yeah, Stephanie was excited about it. She said they needed some alone time." He didn't want to think about his baby sister *that way* so he continued. "We couldn't offer to babysit this time, due to beginning of the school year."

"Well, we got a call."

Again, silence on the other end of the line. Luke was careful not to let his heavy breathing carry over the phone, but now he was shaking.

"Luke, they were in a traffic accident, T-boned, just outside of San Jose. Stephanie was brain dead, no signs of life, no chance, and then she passed. Colin was, well, he was killed instantly."

Luke's veins filled with ice water. It was absolutely the last thing he ever thought he would hear. His little sister, the mother of three beautiful children and whose wedding he was best man for, was gone. She was such a sweet person, such a vibrant soul. And Julie's brother, Colin Christensen, had been one of his best friends when they lived in San Diego. A really solid guy. On board with the big family and hoping to have more.

The four of them as couples had been very close; the cousins—all girls ranging in ages from ten to six—were even closer. Now there were going to be three children without a mother and a father. Aging grandparents, also grieving. It was the worst that could happen, absolutely the worst.

He felt the foundation he'd been building, all the work he'd been doing, begin to crumble. It set him on the dark path he thought he'd recovered from.

"Oh, Dad, I'm so sorry," he said through his tears. "We'll get up there. We'll bring the girls if it isn't too much on everyone."

"No. That's fine."

Mr. Christensen was trying to be strategic, but his thought processes were failing. He was going through the motions, trying to inform, give details, but Luke felt his pain, his utter devastation. It was something he recognized easily with his own struggles with depression and PTSD.

"What do you need right now, and what can I do to help until I get there?"

"Reverend Dobson has been here already, or I'd have called sooner. I know Colin and Steph have a will and a family trust. I just have to find everything. You could help with that if you come. They have all kinds of papers and things, you know. There's the house. I mean, Melinda and I, we just don't know what to do with everything, and it's just such a terrible tragedy. We don't know where to start. No parents should ever outlive their children. And to see your grandchildren filled with pain…"

"Do they know yet?" he asked.

"No, we were going to tell them this evening. Tonight, the kids were supposed to come home. I'm sure it's going to be on the news. I just don't know how we're going to be able to keep it from them. So we'll tell them tonight, and I think, if you came up with the kids, maybe being around their cousins would be a good thing. If you can arrange it."

"Oh, absolutely. We could come right now—"

"No, I know parent-teacher night is an important event for a school principal, and Julie should be there. Once that's over, when she comes home, you can tell her. But don't spoil her evening. There really isn't anything she can do right now. I know she'll want to tend to Melinda. That will be great comfort to her to have her daughter close by."

"We'll hop in the camper van and come on up there. Probably tomorrow morning, but I have to talk to Julie first. How have the kids been? I'll bet they had a great time. You probably spoiled them to death."

"Oh, you know us, Luke. That's our job, our mission in life. The business, Colin's part of it, that will all sort itself out, but it's the kids and all the things that Stephanie and Colin wanted for them, we're going to have to figure that out."

"Knowing Colin, he organized all that down to the last detail. But we'll help any way we can."

He knew it was all in their will. The four of them had even discussed it several times. He knew it would mean moving the three girls down to San Diego. But Luke also considered what Mr. Christensen's reaction to that would be. Here he had just lost his son and daughter-in-law, and now he would be losing the proximity to his grandkids. Even though Luke and Julie lived in San Diego, it was still Southern California, a good ten-hour drive plus. Mr. and Mrs. Christensen's lives that centered around Colin, Stephanie, and the grandkids in Sonoma County were going to be disrupted.

But at least it was still California.

Amy and Jessica came in from the backyard, dripping water all over the kitchen floor. He didn't have the heart to yell at them. Instead, he grabbed a couple of towels and demanded they shed their suits and clean up the water. Sending them up to their room without telling them the news, Luke focused on preparing a good dinner, spaghetti and meatballs, which was their favorite.

He picked lettuce, tomatoes, and a couple cucumbers from the garden and had already made the meatballs and the pasta. At the last minute, he put in a frozen berry pie he'd bought. After the pasta was cooked, he covered it with the homemade tomato sauce using his secret stash of frozen herbs—leftover from making his own herbed vinegar. The heady basil, thyme, oregano, and spearmint added a wonderful flavor to his legendary sauce. He was a real Martha Stewart these days, and it gave him a chuckle, a brief release from the heaviness in his heart.

Cooking for the family had been Luke's job in between deployments. He was Mr. Mom when he was home. Things had been tight, but they were planning on having him quit the Teams and find something local, even perhaps work in an internship for a physician's assistant with his background and training as a medic.

He pondered the changes about to consume them. He remembered the long talks they'd had with Stephanie and Colin by firelight on their numerous camping trips together with all the girls. Each had agreed that, if something happened to the two of them, the other couple would take the children.

Luke had never thought it would happen this way. He always thought the odds were that something would happen to him and Julie would need help with the kids. It never occurred to him that Stephanie and Colin would be the ones to meet a tragic end.

After he put the spaghetti and the sauce in the oven to stay warm, he made some French bread, finding odd comfort in chopping garlic and melting butter. He left part of his insides enclosed behind that iron door— unfortunately, he was too familiar with Dr. Death. That wasn't what would rattle his cage. Right now, he was calm and told himself it was what he was trained for.

*You got this, Luke. You're strong. You've been working full time on this stuff. Going to be a piece of cake...*He told himself all the things some of his buds might say if they were there to comfort him. It was his self-talk.

Their deaths weren't his fault. He wished he'd been there to protect them. And he knew as soon as it popped into his head that idea had to be purged.

Easier said than done.

He was supposed to deploy in two months, and they were working up to a detail in the Caribbean, and perhaps Central America. If he had to re-up, that would be the time to do it so his bonus wouldn't be taxed.

When he'd become a SEAL, he had never thought about what it would be like to have a family, to have people depending on him. He was just a young, dumb, randy, and extremely horny young man, no cares really except getting home from the next deployment or making sure that none of his friends and buddies were left unprotected. His job as a medic was to keep everybody alive and deal with emergencies—surgery, if he had to—but keep them alive until they could be evacuated out of there.

The missions were getting more and more dangerous, although considerably shorter than they used to be ten years ago when he first joined. Julie's career had taken off too. She had worked her way up the ranks to school principal and was in line to perhaps become the district superintendent. That was a discussion they agreed they were going to have soon. His biggest concern before today was how Julie's career might interfere with his job being a Navy SEAL.

But now there was this. A whole new set of decisions to make.

The girls ran downstairs in their flannel jammies. Amy was nine, nearly ten, and Jessica was six.

"Spaghetti!" said Amy. "My favorite!"

Luke studied the two of them, smiling. His precious girls. How their lives would change forever now that their cousins might be coming to live with them. He didn't want to tell them without Julie being present, so he pretended that it was a normal Thursday night—Dad's night to cook spaghetti while Mom worked late.

He served up dinner and enjoyed the banter of his girls' small talk, gossip from school, and comparing notes on some of the new teachers arriving this year. Jessica was in second grade, the same school and grade Julie used to teach. Amy was in fifth grade. Both heavy readers, they were going to be excellent students, Luke could tell. They'd certainly not copy his scholastic achievements.

"Do you have any homework yet?" he asked.

The girls looked at each other and giggled, both of them missing one of their front teeth, on opposite sides, almost looking like twins even with the age difference. They shook their heads no.

"School's just begun, Dad. It's too early!" said Amy.

"I wish I had some homework," sighed Jessica.

"Okay, well, you can watch a little TV tonight if you like. Mom will be home about 8:30 or 9. When she gets here, we'll have a little family meeting and then bed. I want you to brush your teeth and wash your faces, and if you didn't shower, this would be a good time to do that."

"Family meeting?" asked Amy.

"Yes, that's what I said."

"Is Mom going to have another baby?" asked Jessica.

Luke frowned at the comment.

Where the hell did that come from?

"What makes you think that?" he asked.

"Whenever we have a family meeting, it's always something important. Remember when Gramma Christensen got sick with cancer?" Jessica spouted.

Amy shouted back at her. "Stupid. Mom's too old, Jess. She can't have more babies. Her boobs don't work anymore."

Jessica looked at her older sister with admiration, as if she was obviously right in everything. Luke was losing it and nearly burst out laughing.

"I think your mother is going to have to explain a few things to you girls. Things I can't quite do right now. But it is an important meeting."

"Can I read on my iPad?" asked Amy.

"I think you can do that, yes. As long as it's a book, not a TV program. I don't approve you just opening up and watching anything."

"No, it's my app from school, the books we're supposed to read this year."

"Then that's fine with me."

The girls dashed upstairs to their bedrooms, and that's when it hit him. In this small house of theirs, how were they going to fit three more kids in? They would have to share, but Colin and Stephanie's kids were nearly the same age, so more than likely they would have to take one bedroom together, and his two girls would have to share the other spare. He was anxious for Julie to get home so he could start figuring out some of the logistics. He wondered if she would be able to take the day off tomorrow.

Recognizing he was obsessing over little things, he knew this was the beginning of a spiral he didn't want to take. He stopped, took a big drink of ice-cold water, and just stared at the garden, the flowers, and Julie's vegetables. He saw the mess with the water and the pool, but he just observed it, didn't judge it, or get anxious about cleaning it up. He drank another glass of water and began to feel better.

It was a win, after all. The old Luke would have downed a six pack or some whiskey.

'Pick your battles carefully and celebrate all your wins, no matter how small,' Dr. Brownlee had told him.

He cleaned up the dishes, turned on the dishwasher, and had thrown all the dirty towels and bath towels into the washing machine, just about to turn it on, when the front door opened, and Julie returned. She was dressed in her Navy blue suit, looking the part of the professional she was. As she slid off her shoes and set down her briefcase, he was suddenly so grateful and proud of her. She was the best mother and so patient with the girls, and though it was difficult for her at times, she had stood by him in his darkest hours after his difficult deployments and issues with PTSD. He never heard her complain. She was firm and laid boundaries down, but she was always in his corner. That was something he could count on.

"Welcome home, Sweetheart," he said, approaching softly and giving her a hug, holding her tightly, a little longer than usual.

Julie quickly pushed away and stared into his eyes. "Oh my gosh, are you on some new kind of medication or you're just happy to see me?" It took a couple of seconds, but she did break into a quick smile.

"No, I'm just happy to see you." He hesitated. "But, Julie, we have to talk."

He was going to lead her over to the couch to sit down next to her, but she stopped him.

"Luke, what is it?"

He stared down at his feet even as one arm wrapped around Julie's waist, pulling her closer. Looking back into her soft, beautiful face and getting lost in her chocolate brown eyes, he had to tell her the truth. "Julie, Colin and Stephanie have been killed in an auto accident."

He didn't need to say anything more. Her reaction was immediate. Stiffening, she clutched his shirt at his back, almost digging her fingernails into his flesh beneath it. Tears started pouring from her eyes, and she would've leaned over and shouted or screamed, but he held her firm.

"No!"

"Your dad called. And I think it would be a good idea if we went up there this weekend. Tomorrow, if you can make it."

Through her tears, she asked him, "How?"

"I have no idea, Julie, except that they were coming back from that convention in Las Vegas. They were close—in San Jose—and I guess somebody hit them. I didn't get many details, because your dad was pretty upset. He did mention that your mom really needs you."

She wiped her eyes with the backs of her hands, tried to straighten her hair, and adjusted her skirt. She wiggled loose from Luke's arms and removed her jacket, setting it on the back of a dining room chair. At last, she turned toward him, mumbling, "Of course. We'll go tomorrow."

He could see she was all about healing, making things better, comforting her mom. It was amazing she could just do that, Luke thought.

Then another wave of tears hit her as she bent over, the grief overtaking her.

"Oh my God, those poor kids!" she sobbed.

Luke traversed the room and held her in his arms again. He found himself tearing up as well. He remembered his vibrant sister, smiling on her wedding day—the day that brought him and Julie back together again.

"We need to tell the girls," he whispered to the side of her face. "You want to wait until the morning?"

Julie shook her head. "If we're going up tomorrow, I think tonight would give us more time to talk it over and help calm them. Tomorrow, we'll be getting ready for the trip. I'll have to make some calls first, but we'll pack everything up and then head out as soon as we can." Tears filled her eyes again. "Poor mom," she said, beginning to shake, her hand over her mouth.

Luke thought about his parents, both gone now,

and how he was grateful they didn't have to experience the loss of his sister. Stephanie had been their pride and joy.

In a daze, Julie walked over to their living room couch and collapsed, putting her face in her hands resting on her knees.

"Can I get you anything, Honey?"

"I need a whiskey."

"Coming right up."

He brought her a small tumbler with one giant cube of ice. He decided not to join her but sat next to her, holding her left hand.

"How are we going to make this work, Luke? My mind is going crazy. I want to fix this, and there just isn't any way to do that. Of course, the girls have to come here, but we don't have any room. Where will everyone sleep?"

"I know. We'll sort it."

"And we were going to have you leave the Teams. Maybe—"

"Hey, let's take it one step at a time. Let's see what's set up and what we must figure out. I know Colin probably has a bunch of stuff prepared. Let's see what we're facing first and take care of the girls and your folks. Help our girls adjust to it all. Then we can make our minds up. I'll do whatever needs to be done."

"Maybe I should come home—"

"Honey, no. Let's not do this now. We'll figure it out as we go along. The right path will come to us."

She smiled up at him through her tears. Even with her cheeks red and blotchy, her eyelids already getting puffy from the tears, she was beautiful—the most beautiful woman in the world to Luke.

"Look at you, calming *me* down, Luke. I like seeing you strong. This changes everything for us—for all of us."

But then her smile turned into worry, bringing on more tears. He nodded, knowing exactly what she was thinking.

Their family of four was now going to become a family of seven. Money had been tight these past couple of years especially. If one of them quit, how would they be able to make it?

For now, they would be raising not two, but *five* girls.

All their best-laid plans had suddenly flown out the window.

CHAPTER 2

J ULIE WATCHED AS the girls made their way down the stairway, taking a seat on the couch on either side of her. Luke was sitting across from them.

She took a deep breath and began what she hoped would be a speech that would make sense to them. She placed her hands on the tops of their heads, and they leaned into her. She knew they had no idea what was coming next.

"First of all, I'm afraid we've got some bad news."

At that, both girls sat up straight, turned in her direction, and searched back and forth between her face and their dad's.

"What's wrong?" asked Amy.

"What kind of bad news?" asked Jessica, already crying.

Julie drew Jessica to her chest and kissed the top of her head. "Sweethearts, Colin and Stephanie were in an auto accident, and unfortunately, Lindsey, Maron, and

Kiley have lost their parents."

"But where will they go now? Will they live with Gramma and Grandpa?" asked Jessica.

"Well, it probably means they're going to come live with us. We will be sharing our house with your cousins. We want to give them the home that they've lost."

"That would be super cool, Mom. But they must be very sad," Jessica said spontaneously and then buried her head in Julie's side. "Mama, I don't ever want anything to happen to you or Dad."

"I don't think you'll ever have to worry about that, Sweetheart. And it would be a wonderful thing to share your life with them, wouldn't it?"

Jessica nodded, satisfied with the answer.

Amy was curious, wanting all the details, but Jessica was pensive.

"Sweethearts," Luke began. "We're going to go up there tomorrow, and you'll get to see your cousins. We're going to see Grandma and Grandpa, and we'll probably have to stay a few days up there to get things sorted out. I think you will be a great joy to your grandma and grandpa. You could probably help Grandma especially with some of the things she needs to do, and your cousins, they're going to need your love and support. I know I'll be proud of both of you. It's a very sad time for our family, but we are a family, and we are together in this."

"Why wouldn't we move to Santa Rosa? There are three of them and two of us," asked Amy. "They have a huge house."

"No, Sweetheart, I have a job here. Your dad has a job here. San Diego is our home. I don't think it would be a good idea for us to disrupt that at this time," Julie answered. "And your aunt and uncle talked to us about what they wanted if something should happen to them, just as we did for you two. It was all agreed to in advance that if something happened to your dad and me, you both would go to live with Colin and Stephanie. In this case, the opposite happened. And they asked us if we would raise their girls if they weren't here to do it. We gave them our promise and our commitment. We are family, and we will stick together. We don't want the girls to not have a loving home, do we?"

Both girls shook their head back and forth and agreed with Julie.

"Tomorrow is going to be a busy but important day. We want to make sure we talk about this. I'd like to hear what your thoughts are about it, and tomorrow morning when we get up, we're going to pack a few things for a few days, and we're going to leave and drive up there in the camper. It will be like most trips we've taken. And you know there's a lot of things we must do to get ready for it. Mama's going to take a few days off, and Dad's going to let the team know, and we'll gas up and go. You know Grandma and Grandpa are going to be so happy to see you both. And so are your cousins."

"So this is your chance to ask questions," Luke added.

"Will I be sharing my bedroom with Kiley or Maron or Lindsey?" asked Jessica.

"Yes, I think you will share your bedroom with someone. Maybe initially you and Amy will stay together in Amy's room."

"So our cousins will take my bedroom then?" Jessica continued. Julie picked up a little bit of territorial insecurity on Jessica's part.

"It's just a guess. We haven't worked it."

"Are they going to go to our school then?" asked Amy.

"Yes, I think they will, and it will be good for them to have you there to introduce them to all the kids there. I think that Jessica and Kiley might be in the same class, but I'm not sure. You and Maron probably will be as well. It'll be important that you are good ambassadors, and you can really help them in this difficult time by being good friends, sharing all the great things about living here in San Diego with them, so they can begin to have a new life and enjoy living here even though we know they're going to miss their home and parents and everything they had in Santa Rosa."

Julie's heart was breaking at the expression she saw on both her daughters' faces. They were trying to be brave, but Jessica was having a hard time with her lower lip and the steady stream of tears from her eyes.

"What else do you have questions about?" she asked.

"Will Grandma and Grandpa come live with us too?" asked Amy.

Julie looked at Luke, who all of a sudden had a puzzled look on his face.

"That's something I've never thought about, Amy. I don't think so, but of course, they'd be welcome. They'd have to sleep in the backyard in a tent though." Julie kept her demeanor straight, and several seconds later, both the girls giggled, catching the joke.

Luke inserted, "There're going to be lots of things we have to decide and work out. And we're going to ask that you be patient with us and just understand that your mom and I are going to do everything we can to take care of your cousins and to include them in our family, and we may make some mistakes, but we're going to work really hard to try to make this work."

Julie was concerned that the girls weren't more talkative, but she understood they were still processing.

Amy still had not shed a tear. Julie suspected she'd be crying herself to sleep.

Both she and Luke tucked the girls into their bed, and Jessica asked if she could sleep in the same bed with Amy, who agreed. Luke read them a short story while they began to doze off, the sniffling and crying subsiding. Finally, little Jessica rolled over to the side holding her teddy bear and was fast asleep before the story was finished. He leaned over and kissed Amy on the forehead and gave Jessica a peck on the cheek.

Julie was proud of her warrior husband, the one who had learned to adjust more than she did, finding the space and the capacity to help the family now that this crisis had begun. She loved him even more watching how tenderly he loved the girls.

They stayed up for an hour talking over different scenarios and throwing out different ideas. Luke said he would give Kyle a call in the morning and try to figure out some way he could get some time off, perhaps miss the next deployment, if it was deemed necessary. All talk of her quitting her job Luke stopped mid-sentence and wouldn't let her speak about it.

"You've worked too hard, Julie, to get here. My days on the Team are going to be numbered anyway. I'm an old man now with sore knees and a sore back. I shouldn't be doing this kind of work much longer, but whatever we need to do, we'll do it. I'll adjust."

She was grateful for the man she'd met that night on the beach in San Diego. He'd been in a state of grief over the loss of his friend from their last mission, and he had worked hard to hold himself together, to get the treatment, and to not give up on himself in the process.

"You've worked hard to get to where you are as well, Luke. It doesn't seem right for me to ask you to quit the Teams. To do what? Be Mr. Mom?"

"Well, it's not that bad."

She knew he was lying through his teeth.

"You are a terrible liar. Come on, Luke, you never thought of yourself as being a professional babysitter, Mr. Mom full-time. You didn't even like changing diapers when they were little."

"Whew! I did it, though. You have to admit, it was a humbling experience."

She laughed at that.

"My hero. Always there. Always protecting the innocent. Little did you know that your protection detail would expand so."

"Comes with the package. It's what I do."

The next morning, they packed up their camper van and headed north for the ten-hour trip to Sonoma County. It was quiet. Amy didn't want to read. Both girls sat in their seats, staring out the window. Luke made several attempts to tell jokes or funny stories, which fell flat.

At dusk, they finally arrived in Santa Rosa. Julie's mother ran from the front door to the van, her face in a wide smile, focusing her attention on the girls. They hugged then the girls took off, almost bypassing their grandfather on the way to the house to greet their cousins. The three girls were standing in the doorway, none of them smiling.

Julie hugged her mom. "How are you holding up?"

"I'm finding the strength. The girls have been a life-saver. To be honest with you, I've welcomed the distraction of fussing over them. It's been good for me. I'm glad you're here, though, because there're so many decisions that have to be made, and I just don't know what to do." She frowned and then sobbed softly. "I go fine for a while, and then an hour later, I'm crying again. I think that's normal, but the girls are quiet. A little too quiet. And, Julie, I'd like you to talk to them if you could please. I know they have some questions they probably don't want to ask me. They miss their mother."

"I planned on it."

"I know you and Luke are going to be good for them. If there's anything we can do to help, in any way we can, we'd love to. Your dad and I have talked, and if the girls need any financial help at all, we would be happy to contribute."

Julie knew her father was planning on retiring this

year and giving his business to Colin, who had moved from San Diego several years ago to do so. All that would have to be on hold now.

"Mom, don't worry about all this. We'll sort it out. The main thing is we're all together and we're family."

All five of the girls were laid out in the upstairs guest bedroom, where Mr. and Mrs. Christensen had a double-sized bunk bed so that the girls could sleep close together. Amy and Lindsey took the top bunk, and Maron, Kiley, and Jessica took the bottom bunk. They ordered pizza, tried to keep the language upbeat, and turned in early.

After the girls fell asleep, Luke and Julie and her parents had a sit down and discussed the funeral arrangements.

"They used our attorney, Edmond Anderson, and I've got his office putting together the copy of their will. I'm supposed to get that tomorrow. I think he set something up with a funeral home, but not sure. He said he would bring it by. There's the house, there's some savings, and Stephanie had her little side business, her little cosmetic business, which I don't think she was doing much with anymore. I sure am going to miss Colin at the office." Her dad sighed.

"Let's wait to see what Mr. Anderson says when he comes, and hopefully, he'll sit down and go over all the provisions in the will," said Julie.

Her mother brought out a questionnaire that the funeral home had given them. "They have all these packages—" Julie's mother couldn't continue.

Luke inserted himself. "You know, I don't think any of us are up to this right now. Let's just turn in, and let's deal with it tomorrow. It's not going to make any difference. I don't feel like dealing with this right now, and I don't know how the rest of you feel, but this is just not something I want to do. Let's wait. I think that's best."

Julie agreed.

Julie and Luke took Julie's old bedroom, and a flood of memories growing up in this house came back to her. She remembered her first prom night, her first kiss on a date, the first time she had someone up to her room to listen to music and do homework. She used to sneak a kiss here and there. She remembered getting ready to go off to college and saying goodbye to her room, knowing that something was about to change in her life. When she came back for vacations and during school breaks, she had felt she didn't belong but was glad they hadn't re-decorated the room. She remembered the graduation party her parents held for her and roughhousing with Colin in the backyard, playing football with some of his friends before he moved down to San Diego.

Julie had followed him down there and got her first

teaching job after she got her degree.

There had been a lot of happy memories in this room, and she found those memories helped her heal right now. And with Luke's presence, it was easier for her to face her future. He was the man she'd always dreamt she would marry. He was strong and fiercely loyal, and he worked very hard to repair himself and to get help with his PTSD, making huge strides.

They had just begun to level out to the point where they could consider maybe living on one income so that Luke could stay home and take care of the girls or take a regular job that didn't require he be out of the country for huge blocks of time. Something less dangerous perhaps. But she didn't know what he was going to want to do, and right now, it would be hard—especially facing raising all the girls—to only have one income.

As they lay in bed looking up at the reflection of the leaves in the window, Luke put his arm around her and, with his feet sticking out at the bottom of her bed, said, "You know, I've never spent a night in this room before, Julie? I kind of feel like I'm the cat that ate the canary. I sort of feel like I'm in high school, and I snuck into your room or something."

"You're being silly. Really silly, Luke."

"But your parents... I feel like I have to be quiet, try not to snore. Like having sex would be forbidden." He laughed. "Yeah, I am being silly. But I'm having to think about things I'd forgotten a long time ago."

Julie suddenly was concerned perhaps he was pulling back memories of his first wife, Camilla, and their unborn baby, who'd been killed in a car Luke was driving. She was on alert to stop him in case it led to some of those dark, guilt-ridden places he'd found it hard to dig out of.

"Well, we planned for this, Luke. It's why we had all those conversations. Think of how bad it would be if we hadn't done that. We didn't know if we'd ever need that plan, but we made the promises and commitments."

He hesitated for a few moments and then answered, "Whatever we need to do, I'm going to do it. I know I can do it."

"We need to be realistic, Luke. I don't think it's going to be in the cards for you to quit. And if you re-up, you get a bonus, so that might help, but I just want to make sure it's what you want to do. I will quit my principal job if you're going to continue on the Teams."

"So if I decide to stay in, you're going to give up your career?"

"Not exactly, probably not permanently, but maybe temporarily."

"I'm going to have to take that into consideration.

That kind of puts a little more pressure on me. You make a lot more money as a principal than I do as a SEAL. I could find something else to do."

"Like what?"

"I could join the police force, Sheriff, private security. There's lots of stuff I could do. Fitness training, security consulting for corporate groups, helping kids get ready for BUD/S training or military service."

"Okay, those all work. But it's going to be a full-time job taking care of these kids. They're at the age where they have things they're going to want to do, softball, soccer, dance—whatever. I'm not exactly sure what all the three girls are going to want. It sort of requires that somebody be home on a regular basis."

"I got it. And that's what I'll be. Mr. Joe Regular."

My Navy SEAL husband a Joe Regular? She couldn't help but chuckle then tried to hide her amusement.

"What? You don't think I can adjust?"

"I know you can't adjust that much. Throw down your body armor for an apron? Seriously, Luke, you think that will work?"

"Try me!"

Julie knew this line of discussion wasn't going to get her anywhere. His stubbornness was a strength on the Teams, and yes, he'd been trained to be adaptable, to a point. But to shift his whole focus to doing housework and shuttling kids around San Diego County?

That was a different skillset, and he wasn't trained in that. And if he gave up something he loved doing so much for something that could put him over the edge, was that smart?

"I mean it, Julie. You can depend on me to do whatever it takes. I will make this work. I will have the cleanest house, the best-dressed girls, the most on-time taxi, and join the ranks of stage mom, soccer mom, whatever is required."

Although she wasn't convinced it would work, she loved it when he talked about wearing an apron and nothing else. And that gave her other ideas.

She rolled over in the small full-sized bed, pressing herself against his hard body, front to front, and whispered, "So let's see how adaptable you can be. Make love to me without waking my parents or the girls, Luke. Please?"

CHAPTER 3

OLIN AND STEPHANIE'S attorney went through the provisions of the will that had been created, confirming the arrangements to have Luke and Julie care for the three children. Everything else was rather mundane. A good friend of Stephanie was going to handle the sale of the house, unless the Christensens or Luke and Julie objected and wanted to occupy the property. The assets would be left in care of the children for their health and safety but under the full control of Luke and Julie.

Luke had no idea what the estate was worth. Colin did have some savings, stocks, and shares of his father-in-law's firm, but most of the assets were tied up in the house. He was uncomfortable with the idea that Mr. and Mrs. Christensen were left out of the equation. Their loving selflessness had been demonstrated over the years toward all of them. He made a note to discuss with Julie, if they could, his desire to perhaps leave something to them, as her dad was planning to retire this next year. Now, without Colin, he might have to work a few years longer. Maybe they could help them too, without taking anything from the girls.

"Basically, what we have here is a pretty straight-forward will and the trust. Julie, you are executor. You can make the decision where the children are to live, whether you move up here or they come down there to San Diego, and if you want to occupy their house here in Sonoma County or want it sold and the assets applied to the children's welfare. You basically have free rein, as long as you don't co-mingle the funds with your own personal funds. Now having said that, I realize that's sometimes a tricky proposition. So I'm going to request, and it's voluntary but recommended, that we have an annual meeting to go over what monies from the trust have been spent. I'd like to do this up until the time they're old enough to inherit their portion, but you can discontinue at any time. It was Colin and Stephanie's express condition that the children not inherit a large sum of money until they're at least twenty-five, unless it's applied to college tuition or a training program."

Luke affirmed that Colin was as anal as he suspected he would be. He secretly thanked his lucky stars it wasn't the other way around, because his finances were a complete mess. Even with Julie's promotion to principal, they were living paycheck to paycheck. He'd never been very good at managing money, but he was going to have to learn. Of course, now they were hopefully going to have the money to manage.

The other issue that became clear to him was that the choice to leave the teams was now a real issue. He was hesitant to make the decision today with everything else going on, but he knew it would be the first thing he and Julie needed to discuss.

"My office is available any time you have a question. Of course, we bill you for it, but it's a lot cheaper if you ask a question rather than wind up doing something that might find scrutiny either with the tax man, the federal government, or an interested party. I don't anticipate the two of you will have any problems, however."

Julie accepted the records, statements from bank accounts, and mortgage statements in a huge manilla envelope labeled: Christensen Trust. They could hear keys jangling at the bottom. He then handed Julie a preliminary title report to the beautiful custom home Colin had designed and finished not more than a year ago. It was a stunning architectural masterpiece on five acres.

Luke was wary. Because it was Colin's and Stephanie's home, even if Julie and the kids wanted to live there, Luke would not be able to do so. It creeped him out.

Mr. and Mrs. Christensen agreed to watch the kids for a short while so Luke and Julie could stop over at the house and be alone for a private discussion. Luke was nervous even stepping foot in the house, almost as if it was a bad omen or stepping on a person's grave. He hoped they could be quick, grab a light snack and some good strong coffee, and be back at the Christensen house within minutes.

On the way, Luke got a call from Kyle.

"Finally, Landmine. I was beginning to wonder whether the team deployed and I somehow missed the flight," Luke barked.

"Well, I'm sure if you guys have a couple more kids you'd understand how it feels to have three. They sure keep us busy. And, Christy? Well, if it wasn't for the kids, she'd probably ignore me and work twenty-four seven. She is so busy these days."

Kyle did make a good point. There was a way for a Navy SEAL to be married to a career-oriented working woman without the kids suffering. Ye, Kyle was always to the point of exhaustion every time he had to spend the whole day or two with them without any help from his spouse.

But Kyle's comment about the kids hit Luke the wrong way. Managing three was one thing. Managing five quite another. But it irritated him all the same, and he couldn't let go of it. He warned himself that it wasn't a good idea to react to his LPO.

Kyle coughed into the phone. "So what's up, Luke? You said you had something personal to talk to me about?"

"I didn't want to tell you on the phone, but Colin and Stephanie were killed in an auto accident two days ago. We've just come up here to Sonoma County, and I was trying to give you a call letting you know I was going to miss a couple of days of PT."

"Oh, Geez. I'm so sorry, Luke. My condolences to Julie, the girls, and Mr. and Mrs. Christensen too. You all must be devastated."

"It's hard on all of us."

"Of course it is."

"We need to stay up here with Julie's mom and dad, because there's a lot we have to decide. Julie's the executor of their estate. Accounts have to be closed, safety deposit boxes opened, funeral arrangements made, and all their things organized. It looks like we'll be bringing the three girls back home with us."

"Oh, wow, where have I been? I didn't realize they had three. That's a shame. How did it happen?" Kyle asked.

Out of nowhere, Luke was suddenly furious with his LPO. His anger flared as his body began to sweat. His blood pressure exploded. Before he could take control of himself, he went straight into attack mode.

"Why does everyone fucking want to know what happened?" He felt the familiar irritation like an old grudge against some imaginary villain. It was uncharacteristically aimed at Kyle, but it was more like he was angry with the whole world for being lopsided, for leaving him alive to experience it all.

"Wait, Luke, that's—"

"Everyone wants the gory details. They were killed, smashed up. They died. He went right away, and my baby sister lingered and was brain dead and then died."

Just then, he noticed he wasn't alone. Julie was sitting right next to him and had heard every nasty word. Luke had gone off-planet, way into the Twilight Zone.

Julie urgently motioned for him to pull over, and he shook his head, waving her off.

"I said, pull over, Luke."

Instead of stopping, he handed her the cell phone. "You talk to him." Before she could speak to Kyle, Luke squeezed the steering wheel and shouted "Fuck!"

Julie jumped right in and nervously tried to save the communication like he used to when they first began dating. "I'm sorry, Kyle. He's been doing great. He really has. We drove all day yesterday getting up here. Today, well, it's been a long, painful day. We're all stressed. This is going to be a big change for us—all of us. I know it sounds selfish, but please give him a little bit of time to work it out. We don't know exactly what we're going to do. But he needs some time to figure it out. None of us want to rush into anything."

She held the phone from her ear so Luke could hear what Kyle had to say.

"I see. Well, I'm glad you're there, Julie. Because that didn't sound at all healthy coming from Luke. I have great sympathy for what you all are going through. I don't know who the fuck was that guy I just talked to, but I'm going to forget about it and just hope and pray he gets to a meeting or talks to Brownlee, something. Don't let him dangle with all this shit. And I don't want him saying something to me I have to report."

"Understood. I'll tell him."

"And I apologize if I reacted harshly. You take all the time you need. Have him call me when he's got some of this sorted. And, Julie, we're all here so sorry about this. If there's anything you need, you just let me know. When you get back, Christy and the ladies are going to be all over you guys. Hope you don't mind, but it's what we do."

"I know it. I'm grateful."

"Luke's mental health is important to me. Until he decides to go off the Teams, he's my responsibility. So make sure he gets help—lots of help. He's not going to like you insisting, of course, because that's the way we're wired, but you make sure he gets help up there."

"I certainly will. Thank you. We'll be in touch."

Kyle hung up.

Luke had heard every single word Kyle said. He completely agreed with his LPO. And he'd just made a huge mistake. The anger came without warning, out of nowhere. Like all of a sudden, he was unbalanced, capable of doing anything, and that scared him big time. He knew what it was. He knew the feelings that he had inside, the survivor's guilt, and knew it came from a place of not being well. Sick people focus on themselves. Healthy people focus on everybody else and try to make things better. He knew he was going to have to fucking suck it up and get his shit together right away or he would lose everything: his career, his wife, maybe even his whole family.

"I screwed up, Julie. I'm sorry."

Julie set his phone in the holder up by his right hand and crossed her arms. He could feel her irritation.

"I'm not going to lie to you. That was very unfortunate."

"You think? I'm shocked at how fast it came upon me."

"Yeah, well, that's what the doctor told you. That means that you have more work to do."

"But I've—" He started to object.

Now it was Julie's turn to get upset. She turned in

her seat to face him.

"There it is again, Luke. You have to understand that's coming from a place that's only in your mind, doesn't exist. You need to talk to someone, even more than before. We don't want this to spin you out."

She placed her hand on his arm.

"I'll be with you. We'll do this together. Don't shut me out, even if you think I've done something you don't like, because all I'm doing is caring for you, loving you. But I have a lot on my plate, too, with all these decisions. I need you whole and beside me. Do that for me. I think the rest will take care of itself. And don't reject Kyle's suggestions. I know you don't like it, but he's right. You even said he was right. He's your best friend in the whole world. You need him, too, Luke. Don't push us away now."

Luke was filled with regret. But that was part of the symptom of his PTSD. Everyone screws up, he thought to himself. He needed to stop beating himself up over it. He needed to be present.

"I'm going to try harder. You see things coming off the rails, if I don't see it, you point it out and remind me, okay, Julie?"

"Understand you don't have to suffer alone, Luke. I'm right there beside you. No matter what, just like you'd do for us, I won't abandon you. I'm here for you always. Do the best you can, and I'll try to meet you in the middle. That's all I ask, Sweetheart."

Luke felt his anger organize. He put it in a box, like he'd been trained, and double-wrapped it in duct tape, and saw it go smaller and smaller until it was filed away somewhere out of his frontal cortex.

"I know that you are hurting—we are hurting—but right now, the girls are the most important thing. We BOTH have to be strong. We lost two of the most important people to us, but those girls lost their entire world. Until we can give them a firm foundation, we have to hold it together. So get your anger out now before your grief consumes you. Then we go back to being the strong protectors our five little girls need."

Luke's eyes began to water until he sucked in air so deep his lungs hurt. But it made the tears stop, and that was the one thing he wanted to do. She was a hundred percent right. He'd been feeling victimized, not by any one person, but by the world in general.

"How did I manage to marry someone so perfect when I'm so flawed?" he asked her.

He was fully aware that life gave all kinds of lemons to all kinds of people, and it was his fucking turn. But it wasn't fair to make everybody else have to carry his weight like the boat crews on Coronado. Like those jerks, the VIP SEALs, reviewing the BUD/S training, never pulling their weight, and always made it harder for everybody else around them to get any task done when they were on a team. That wasn't going to be the guy he was.

"You're not flawed. You've seen things most people never see, and it's affected you. But you can heal. You have been healing. I'm so proud of you, Luke. Just remember that when you get feeling down. We love you dearly and are all proud of you—all of you."

She began to tear up. "Now our reality and focus will be taking care of my brother's children as well as our own. Five little girls need us, Luke, and like I told you yesterday, I like feeling your strength. That's the Luke I love and the Luke that I married."

He wished he hadn't taken her there, worried about his mental state, but he needed to be honest with himself about his fragility. Thinking about that made the tears stop again. He'd been slipping a little, not carrying his load. Time to man-up and find gratitude in his day. Be humble enough to ask for help.

He was going to be solid. Absolutely rock-hard solid.

"Julie, I'm going to ask for your forgiveness. When I get some time to myself, I'm going to call Dr. Brownlee and see if he can schedule a phone appointment with me."

"You do that, Luke. So glad to hear that, Sweetheart."

They turned to drive up to the subdivision where

Colin and Stephanie's house was, winding up the gentle hillside until they reached the top where the property was. The beautiful copper-roofed home was extremely modern and looked like something Frank Lloyd Wright could have designed, utilizing lots of granite blocks, colored metal window frames, and the copper roof and gutter throwing a golden patina almost as if it was lit up from underneath all over the outside of the house. Attractive lighting here and there highlighted some of Stephanie's prize roses and their professionally landscaped front and side yards. Luke was surprised to see a light on in the home.

They parked in the driveway. Carmen, the lady who lived next door, the street gossip, immediately ran over to Julie and gave her a hug. She was an overweight Pacific Islander or Filipino woman dressed in a bright muumuu, and she'd been barefoot in her front yard watering her colorful flowers.

"Oh, Julie, I am so sorry. If there's anything I can do for you, please let me know," the neighbor said.

"Thank you. We have a lot to think about, but thank you. We're just going to go look around a little bit, and I'll let you know okay?"

Luke wondered how Carmen had found out about their accident. So he decided to ask her. "Is it in the news already?"

"Oh, yes, front page of the paper. Everybody's been

out on their driveways talking about it. The paper said it was a car accident, is that right?"

"Yes, it was."

"When is the funeral? We'd all like to come pay our respects."

Julie sighed, nodding her head. "Yes, of course. We'll make sure you get the details. Probably Monday, but we're still waiting to make the final arrangements."

"Lovely couple. And those darling children. You know, I asked Stephanie if she wanted me to help her clean house or do anything. I don't know how she did it. She had those three girls, and she had her mail order business going on. She's just amazing. And Colin, so handsome and so talented."

She had her hands together clasped over her heart. Luke was having a hard time keeping his shit together watching her performance, which was the only way he could classify what she was doing.

But of course, Julie took it in stride.

"Excuse me, Carmen, but we only have a few minutes, so if you don't mind, we'll talk to you later."

She was much better at this than he was. He was going to have to learn to temper his irritation, because everything in the whole world irritated him. Just being alive irritated him.

He followed behind Julie as she dug into the manila envelope that contained the keys, some other small handheld pieces of equipment, a cell phone for her business and such. Finding the key to the front door at the bottom, she opened it and, after Luke stepped in, closed it behind him.

The large foyer was two stories tall, and the sound of their footsteps on the polished concrete floor, even though covered in exquisite oriental rugs, made him feel like he was at church. Light poured in from stained glass windows on the second floor, creating a Scrabble-type design below. They heard sounds of birds and airplanes outside, a lawnmower, a leaf blower, and other things indicative of a normal early afternoon in California.

Being in the house was hard for Luke. Especially since everywhere he looked he saw the attention to detail that was so much a part of Colin and Stephanie's lives. They walked through the kitchen and found two coffee cups, one with lipstick on the edge, still sitting in the sink, rinsed but not put in the dishwasher. Evidence that they had been together here, sitting, having coffee, not knowing their lives would be cut short.

The beds were made. The fireplace in the family room was clean and stacked with wood. Even the carpets had been freshly vacuumed. Someone had placed fresh flowers on the dining room table, obviously their housekeeper, welcoming them home.

Julie didn't say a word, just walked slowly from

room to room, down the stairs, out onto the patio, and sat on one of the stone retaining walls overlooking Stephanie's garden.

"Such a beautiful place here. They were so happy. The girls... oh my God, Luke, how can we possibly provide anything that looks anything like this down in San Diego for them?"

Luke knew exactly how she felt. Trying to be helpful, he said, "Well, that's not really what makes a home, is it, Julie? It's the people in it. It's not how big it is or where it is or how fancy it is. Even though everyone wants a beautiful house decorated tastefully in a lovely setting to honor who they are. I think our house is beautiful. Small but beautiful. I'm going to say something that you probably won't understand."

"What?"

"I'd rather live in our house than this house."

"Oh, I understand that completely," she said. "I do. I get what you're saying."

"Okay, so the question's going to be for us, what do we want our new family to look like? Does this mean we buy something else, or we somehow remodel our place and make it into something that would suit everybody?"

"God, Luke, there's no room. I mean what do we do, add a third floor?"

"Yeah, maybe it's a project we can talk about later. I

don't know how we'll do it. But if we can somehow stay where we are, keep our expenses just like they were, and use the money that Stephanie and Colin have in the house to help the girls with their college and their lessons and anything else they want, I think we would be okay. I think that's what they'd want us to do. They didn't choose us because we had a great big house on a fancy hill. Steph wanted the girls to be down to earth, not spoiled. They chose us because of how we live our life, Julie."

She immediately stood up and ran to him, wrapping her arms around him so tight while she sobbed into his chest.

"That's my Luke. I needed to hear that, Luke. You're so right. Thank you."

CHAPTER 4

JULIE WAS TO meet with several realtors to give her an opinion of value for Steph and Colin's house. She asked her dad to come along with her, because he was the most qualified to explain the architecture, the design elements, and the features of the house, because he had helped Colin draw up and engineer the design.

One by one, different brokers stopped by, an hour apart, giving their opinion of value and getting the grand tour. Out of the four that she met with, one of them didn't want to give her a price, wanted to call it in the next day. But from everybody else, she got detailed market comps, which is what she was looking for. The prices had risen dramatically since her days in Sonoma County, but more or less fell in line with what Julie had guessed they would be.

In between the appointments, she'd brought some sandwiches and soft drinks for her and her father to sit at the dining room table and wait for the next interviewee.

"You know, Dad, one of the things we might need to do is remodel the house in San Diego. Just so we could accommodate all the girls. It won't look anything like this, but maybe you could help us come up with some kind of a plan that would make sense."

"Boy, I don't know, Julie. You've got a tiny lot there, as most of those are, and you already have a two-story. I'm not sure how much coverage they'll allow you there in San Diego, but I'll take a look and see what I can dig up as far as the zoning and building codes, especially the setbacks. It would honestly be easier to just scrape the lot and start from scratch. You could get a much bigger house out of it. But I also think it would cost you a lot of money."

"Well, that's in short supply, Dad. And of course we don't want to touch the money that goes to the girls. Until the house sells, as a matter of fact, we're going to be very tight. But I think we'll do okay."

Mr. Christensen looked at her admiringly. "You know, Julie, we never doubted you were going to be a great teacher, and now look at you, an administrator, a school principal. I'm so proud of you, and I think you and Luke are going to make wonderful parents to those girls. It's amazing to see how close they are, and now they'll get to live together, which is what they'd always wanted. Remember when they used to beg for this?"

Julie did have fond memories of the tears shed when their visits were over, all the girls begging to be able to go live with their cousins. It was ironic that it was now going to come to pass. But she had to tell him her doubts.

"Well, their time together was special, because in the past, they only got to have face-to-face contact two or three times a year, Dad. If they're going to be living together in our small house, I don't know how exciting or happy it'll be. But we aim to make it work. Trust me on that."

"Good enough then."

After she and her dad concluded their interviews, she picked one particular broker, even without a callback from the broker who didn't have an opinion of value yet. She chose a young aggressive agent who seemed eager and was very experienced selling high-end properties. And, more importantly, she'd sold the neighbor's property. She didn't come in the highest recommended price, but Julie felt she wasn't afraid to tell her the truth, either. Not wanting the house to sit a long time unsold, she wanted to be realistic, gather a lot of attention, and maybe obtain multiple offers.

She exchanged email addresses with the young agent and promised to sign the listing as soon as she got the paperwork. But she also needed to make sure Luke was on board with it.

Julie did a rough calculation of the proceeds. With a listing price of $1.7 million minus the mortgage of eight hundred thousand and funds set aside for three college tuitions at two hundred thousand each, times three, that would leave, by Julie's estimation, roughly three hundred thousand for the girls needs growing up, placed in a trust and managed but spent frugally. She was going to double-check with the realtor the next day, because the realtor had picked up a business loan that had been placed against the property recently, and there was no evidence that that had been paid off.

But these were her rough numbers, good enough to have a cogent conversation with her husband.

At home, Luke was talking to Dr. Brownlee upstairs in her former room, so she left him alone until the call was complete. Later, she told him what she was going to list the property for and what they would be netting. She showed him the paperwork.

"Holy cow. That's terrific. The girls are going to be set."

"It's really not a lot of money, Luke. Not much at all. There may be some credit card debt we have to pay off and a car loan, which will be paid off when we sell it. It's a lot of responsibility to manage that college fund, make sure it keeps growing, but I think we could do some proper investing for them. And I'll have to check with the attorney about using some of the funds to enlarge the house to accommodate the girls. But I want to know what you think, Luke?"

He shrugged. "Sounds reasonable. I don't see why not. It is for their benefit. It would be much easier for them and for us if we had at least two more bedrooms. But I don't know where you're going to find them. Let's think about it, Julie. The house probably won't sell right away, but once it gets close to closing escrow, we'll have to make that decision. You should talk to the attorney now, though."

"Yup. I'm on it."

Mr. Christensen hooked up Julie's computer to his Wi-Fi so his wireless printer could print out the contract when it came through. While everything was being printed, she called the other three brokers and informed them of her decision.

Luke added, "One thing we didn't do, Julie, is look at all their stuff. There are clothes in the closets, filled pantry shelves, Steph's china and crystal. Some of it came from my mom and dad."

"Then we should keep those. That's part of your heritage too."

"There is a garage pretty full of boxes—stuff—not as bad as ours, but still pretty full. I think we should line somebody up to help with the move, so we'll be ready when the house sells. Did they have a storage unit or any other place that they used or was everything there at the house?"

"I have keys to two deposit boxes down at the Bank of Sonoma County and a key to a lot I think he kept an old car in. I'm going to try to find that. But I'll check it out. Other than that, I'm not aware of any other location. Colin had a few things at Dad's office, but I think most of everything is at the property."

"Still, it would fill a U-Haul van. That's more than we can handle. I'll get some help when we get down south from the Team guys."

"Good. Oh, and the realtor told me I needed to de-clutter and perhaps get it staged. I told her we'd try to remove some things, but I didn't want to pay to have it staged."

"I think you're right about that. The house is going to sell itself. It's such a beautiful piece of property, and the yard is just stunning."

"We'll arrange a work party, then. Maybe you could contact Zak and Amy, Nick and Devon—see if we can hire out their farm crews to give us a hand."

"I'll give them a call."

"How was your call with Brownlee?"

"He was concerned, and we had a good talk about looking for warning signs. He didn't buy that it came on suddenly, and I didn't have any advance notice. He said I wasn't paying attention and to be more aware of what my body needs. There's no such thing as a flare-up or an anger event occurring without stuff building ahead of time. And the long drive and all the stress, it just added on more layers. I have to be careful about my rest, and I honestly haven't been sleeping well lately."

"I've been a little on edge as well. You're probably like I am, wondering how we're going to make ends meet. The money isn't ours, and I know you know that. But there won't be much coming in until after the house sells. We're going to have to be very careful on what we spend."

Luke agreed with her completely.

"I guess I better call the old man then. Kyle's expecting it. I hope this dustup from yesterday doesn't affect my position on the team. But the fact is, Julie, if I don't stay on the team, if they toss me, so be it. I mean, I'm not going to fight to stay. I want to stay at this point, but now we have some options, and nobody can predict the future. As long as you're working, I think I'd like to try handling the load taking care of all five girls. And that's what I'm going to tell him. So if he won't give me several months off, then I'm going to let him know that I'll start the paperwork to disengage."

"Can I have an opinion about this?" Julie asked.

"Of course. Always. I shouldn't have said it that way. I meant to ask if you agreed with me."

"I think you ought to take a look at what you see

yourself doing. Raising children and being a stay-at-home parent is not the easiest job in the world. I did it off and on, I guess, but this, with all five of them, this is a full-time situation. We could probably get help by using a bit of the money, take some of the stress off of us having to work ourselves to the bone twenty-four seven. But I want you happy, Luke. I don't want any regrets. And if you decide to leave the teams, I don't want you to come back later on and tell me that was a mistake."

"I understand. But none of us knows how this is going to affect us all. I might really take to it, or I might hate it. I don't know. But what I do promise you is that I will give it a good try for several months at least, and I think that's the time I'll make the decision—after I actually see what it's like to not be working out with the guys, getting ready to deploy, go overseas, and then come back. I need to see what that's going to feel like if I can."

"And the beauty of all of this is that Colin and Stephanie have set it up for us so that we do have that choice. That's a blessing. Most people don't have that."

Julie could see her words were hitting home. Luke's eyes were filled to the brim with tears, again.

CHAPTER 5

"SO HOW ARE you, Luke?" his LPO asked. Luke didn't detect any residual frostiness, even though he deserved it.

"I think I'm okay, Kyle. There's a shit pile of decisions we have to make. God, I've got so many lists, and so does Julie. Every hour that goes by, we think of something else we have to do. We put it on the list. Being a teacher, she's good with the visual aids. We got some of those big Post-it notes and started listing things, making categories of decisions, people we had to call, forms to fill out, things to do. We got the funeral arrangements taken care of. We even spoke to the girls' schools and inquired about the school our girls go to in San Diego."

"You guys go to Mission Viejo?"

"No, Bell City. It's a private school. I think the kids are going to love it there."

"Well, it sounds like things are progressing. What

do you think happened the other day?"

"I knew we'd get to that. Julie and I talked about it afterwards, and you need to know, Kyle, she really brought me to my senses. Boy, she's direct."

"I think that's good for you, Luke. You want someone with boundaries. That's gonna save you in the long run when perhaps you forget."

"Oh, definitely. Anyway, she said that I was probably tired from the drive, and neither one of us had been sleeping very well, even before all this happened. Brownlee's backed her up and completely agrees. Being perfectly honest with you, money's been tight. And I've been a little bit worried about my future, whether I want to re-up or whether it's time to get out."

"Well, I'll tell you this, Luke, I would hate to lose you. I need medics. I can do without the bang buddies and some of the communications people. We've got to have sharp shooters and medics."

Luke chuckled. "I remember when Julie asked me why I was also a sharp shooter, and I told her it was just something I was good at. Then she asked, well, are you killing people or are you keeping them alive?"

"What was your answer?"

"A little bit of both, I guess."

"Yeah, that's funny, even though I'm not laughing. Most people would never understand, would they, Luke?"

"That's for damn sure. And I think about not being on the teams, and I just, I don't know if I could handle it. I mean, I've seen a lot of guys go down in flames. I just don't know."

"Yeah, disengaging can be a bitch."

That was putting it mildly, Luke thought.

"Well, I'm not going to press you. But I'd like to keep you on the team. And it sounds like you need some time to get things sorted, taking a note from Julie's conversation yesterday. I think I can sell it to the head shed. Get you some special circumstances temporary detachment. Do you think four or five months is enough?"

"Yeah, I think that would work, but I was hoping for six."

"I'll see what I can do, and I'll let you know. But I know I can get you four or five. After that, I'm not sure, with our recruiting numbers down. People aren't signing up for the military in general, but with these special ops programs, it's worse. Sometimes I think we show too many horribly disfigured vets on social media—it kind of scares the nineteen-year-olds, know what I mean?"

"I do. Not interested in a good death or dismemberment."

"Roger that, Luke. But the reality is that it's very dangerous, and you know they're getting more and more dangerous. We have more and more refinements to the rules of engagement. It's getting to be really hard to do what we do. I'm just waiting for the first team to get nailed with a bunch of lawsuits and investigations by Congress or the military brass, not that we're all choirboys. Knock on wood, that hasn't happened yet. But we're the ones using the lethal force if it's necessary. It's never pretty. But it's necessary. We do what others can't or won't. God forbid we ever stop funding the Teams because it's unfair, too violent, or some shit like that."

"I believe in what we do, Kyle. No worries there. I think we make the world a better place. I just want to make sure the toll it takes on me doesn't destroy me in the process. Julie doesn't want that either."

"What does she want you to do?"

"She wants me to do what is best for me. But she doesn't want me to decide and then change my mind or regret the decision."

"Well, you tell me how that's done successfully, Son. If I had the answer to that one, I'd be rich, filthy stinking rich."

"I think, if the Navy doesn't give me the time, I'll be telling you I need to start the paperwork. So you arranging that is going to make it possible so I can stay."

"And that's exactly how I'm going to sell it, Luke."

The next day, Kyle texted Luke to let him know he had his six months. His LPO said he wanted regular check-ins, and he wanted to hear Luke was talking to Brownlee on a regular basis. As his friend, Kyle said, if he needed anything or felt himself slipping, Luke had to promise Kyle he'd give him a call before all hell broke loose.

Luke was grateful for the wise man who'd been his team leader ever since he joined Team 3. Kyle was legendary. He was tough, but he absolutely cared about every single one of his guys. He knew about their families, their kids. He knew everything between the information he got and Christy got. They were the glue of SEAL Team 3. Kyle was more brother than he could ever have. All of the guys were right there with him too.

Luke wasn't going to do anything to disappoint Kyle. He was the finest warrior Luke had met. If he could be half as good a leader as Kyle was, he wouldn't even consider leaving the military.

Next, Luke began making phone calls, arranging a work party with the help of Nicholas Dunn and Zak Chambers, both former teammates on Team 3. Nick said he could drive a U-Haul down to San Diego and follow the camper van if that was what he needed. Luke didn't want Julie driving on her own so accepted his offer gratefully.

There were six other workmen, field hands of Zak's, who showed up one morning the following week. Luke was beginning to feel more normal. The funeral was over; the operational planning was nearly finished; tasks were distributed to others where they could be. As time distanced him from the tragic events earlier in the month, he found it easier to laugh and enjoyed swearing, getting sweaty and dirty loading boxes, and sorting and removing furniture to get ready for the house sale.

He dropped a file-box sized pink mailer that came from Stephanie's mail order business. Julie had discovered that Stephanie had closed her business account, pulled her website, and stopped her mail order business, but some of the items were still in her garage. When one of the big pink boxes labeled Gardens of Delight fell open, Luke, Zak, Nicholas, and several others whistled as several assorted vibrators, lubrication creams, feather whips, satin handcuffs, and sexual toys rolled out at their feet.

"Holy shit! Your sister and Colin were into this kink?" asked Nicholas.

"Well, this is tame compared to some of the things I've seen, and you know it. But no. I don't even think this belongs to Stephanie. I can't see her using any of this stuff. It's kind of play stuff, not hardcore fetish tools. And I know the difference."

The men laughed.

"Maybe they're Colin's," someone said.

"Well, you fellas do know how they're used, right? It's usually for the couple, together. But give me a break. I don't know what got into her head, but I'm glad she stopped it."

One of the helpers indicated he'd seen some of these items before when his wife had attended a home party where many of these were featured, and his wife bought some.

"You mean like a Tupperware party?" asked Luke. He was throwing things back in the pink box, annoyed that his family's dirty laundry was displayed for all to see.

"With an F. And they don't have to walk into those specialty stores. Some ladies just won't do that," added Nick.

"Exactly," agreed Luke.

Zak needed to add his opinion. "No, it's quite legit, Luke. Girls get together and drink a bunch of wine, and they model skimpy nightgowns and show little things, little toys that are kind of fun. I won't lie. I didn't mind when Amy went. She likes to experiment. It's kind of the rage now," he said.

"Well, if this was her mail order business, no wonder she shut it down. I mean, I wouldn't want the girls to see this crap. Like I said, I wonder what the devil got into her," Luke mused.

"Hey, Man, don't beat yourself up. It's the way things are these days. She was probably just trying to make a few extra bucks on the side. And if it was really taking off, well, I think you'd hear about it, right?" said Zak.

"I suppose. But look at all this stuff, I mean, look at all these boxes. She had a ton of inventory." He pointed to nearly a dozen large square boxes with the flowered designed logo in pink, along with a couple of ledgers she had prepared for sales on top. Luke looked them over before setting them back down on the stack of boxes. He could see that she had a healthy profit every month, stopping just around when they went to Vegas. She was very clearly going to quit, so Luke didn't worry about it, understanding that Stephanie had obviously changed her mind and had been getting out.

"So now what are we going to do with these? We certainly can't turn them into Goodwill," said Nick.

That got another chuckle from the group.

"I wouldn't take them to the county dumps either. You probably would get a ticket for it," added Zak.

"Yeah, that's just what I need, right? I can see it in the papers now, *Navy SEAL and his elementary school principal wife continues sister's sex toys business*. No, we can't have that. I'll find a way to dispose of it. I certainly am not going to leave it in the garbage down at the

Christensen's. If they found one of these boxes, they're liable to have a heart attack."

"So I'll just put them over to the side in the U-Haul then. You want to hang on to these ledgers?" Nick asked as he handed the books back to Luke.

"Yeah, I'll give it to Julie. She probably has to make a note and keep track."

Several days later, the purging had been completed. At the last minute, several of the workmen's wives were called in to wrap, box, and tape things, especially some of the China and crystal, so that they could be transported safely back to San Diego. Mrs. Christensen had been asked if she wanted any of it, and she took a few bowls and a pair of crystal candlesticks, but Colin's mug collection and several of the other pieces they had on display, she didn't have room for. Her husband passed on them as well.

"Needs to go to a beer drinker. Some of these are valuable. You might be able to sell them too."

Luke was going to have to rent a mini warehouse, because their garage in San Diego was already full to capacity, such that they couldn't park their cars in it. But with the help of the estate money, that shouldn't be a problem.

The realtor did a final walkthrough, approving of all the empty closets in the bedrooms and the dishware purge in the kitchen as well as things in the baths. She also indicated that several potted trees and plants should be removed eventually, as there would not be anyone living here to take care of them.

"I'll tell the folks. Maybe they'll want them. We've got the truck completely filled."

The realtor had a landscaper come in and plant extra flowers in Stephanie's flowerbed and trim several of the bushes, and he agreed to a weekly lawn trimming that Colin used to do himself.

With only the bare minimum of furniture left for that lived-in look, things he'd have to come up and remove later or donate to charity, it was ready. He took one long look again, so he could remember this unique place that held their happy family.

"At least you got to build it and live in it for a bit, Colin," he mumbled to his friend. "Good on you. Now it goes to someone else to do the same. You created a masterpiece the next owner will love."

Closing the door behind him, he wasn't sure he'd ever need to come back. The finality of the impending sale created a shudder down his spine. And then he remembered, "You can't take it with you. Nothing belongs to us forever, even our families. Rest in peace, Colin, and give my sis a big hug and kiss."

The house was put on the market the day they left for the return trip to San Diego, stopping by their school one more time so the girls could say goodbye to their classmates and their teachers. There were some tears, but Luke saw in his little family, they were bonding together and helping each other. He was so proud of his girls. They were becoming sisters more and more every day. Lindsey and Amy were inseparable, and Maron and Jessica had formed a close friendship, but Jessica and Kiley were closest in age and had a special bond. He saw them holding hands more times than not. Luke saw a huge future ahead of them all just by watching them learn to be sisters.

It was a bright late morning when the two vehicles hit the road, headed for their new home in Southern California. Luke knew this was going to be the real test.

He was hoping for the best, and he was suddenly optimistic.

CHAPTER 6

JULIE TURNED AROUND to view the five girls sitting on the couch in the back of their Sprinter van. They were reading books, playing on their electronic devices, or coloring on a small table they had bolted to the floorboards. If someone were to watch them, you wouldn't know that, just a couple of weeks before, they lost their parents and now were going to be uprooted, would be attending a different school, living in a different town, and making new friends.

"Would you look at that, Luke?" she whispered to her husband sitting behind the driver's wheel.

"I can see them. I've been watching them, Julie. They're great kids. It feels like it's going to work out." He winked as he glanced over to her and gave her a quick smile. Then with eyes back on the road, he checked his mirrors, making sure they hadn't outpaced Nicholas in the large cab-over U-Haul truck.

"I've been watching Nick also. It's too bad we can't

go faster, but it is what it is," she said.

"Well, theoretically, we could, except we'd probably get four miles per gallon in that beast. They didn't have any diesel trucks, but even with the difference in price, we would save probably a few hundred dollars. If you're okay with it, maybe I can spell him so he can have a nice comfortable ride in a leather seat, sitting next to my beautiful wife." He chuckled, pleased with himself.

"That's nice of you, Luke. I don't mind driving the big truck, though. I did my share of moving in my day. I'm not completely helpless."

"Oh, you don't want to drive that thing. It's filthy, and you can smell gasoline. I was lucky to get it, since it looks like all the moving vans are going east to Texas and Florida these days. It was hard to find one to take us to Southern California. I'm glad we got something."

She scanned the scenery, enjoying the comfortable ride and the huge windows. Above all the traffic, this was going in style, she thought.

"So how are your calls going with Dr. Brownlee?" She'd meant to ask earlier.

"Good. He definitely is a leveling influence on me. Wants me to take up tennis or something else like golf. God, I don't think I have the patience for golf." He shook his head, made one of his legendary faces.

Julie loved him for even considering it. She knew, if

she begged him, he would try.

There had been some issues in the school district she had to spend time on just before they left, and she was anxious to get back to work. If they didn't get in too late, she wanted to report for work tomorrow. Her meteoric rise to principal was nearly unheard of, but she was the most popular teacher in the whole school, and many of the parents who were influential in the choice had had their children tutored or taught by Julie over the years, so she had quite a stash of supporters. The district was making signs they would be looking for a new superintendent, and even though she hadn't applied for the job, they let her know her application would be welcomed. She decided it was time to discuss it with Luke.

"What do you think about that superintendent job? You know it's not as secure as a principal's job, and they often move you around."

"How would that work?"

"It wouldn't. I'd have to tell them that with all the kids, especially now, moving would be a non-starter. But what do you think if I can negotiate it, would you be in favor?"

"I think it would be less taxing on you than your current job, Julie. You know, dealing with all those parents and then the curriculum issues, the personnel problems, and teacher issues. I mean, you have to manage the whole school. You even help decide what they plant and what goes in the playground for heck's sake. I think those superintendents kind of have light duty, and for all the money they make, wow, it's a no-brainer."

"Okay. So why do I think there's a but in there somewhere?"

"This is what I really worry about," he said as he looked at her carefully. "I worry that it would be too distanced from teaching. Like I'm not sure any of our superintendents have actually been long-term teachers. They come from a management background, a curriculum background, or even a publishing background for some of them. I'm not sure that's what really sets your heart on fire. You like being with the kids."

"But it would give me the opportunity to perhaps help formulate the direction that our schools would go in, and I'd have more resources available to me. I wouldn't have to be distant if I chose not to. It's just some of those superintendents are careful, so careful about not making favorites that they wind up appearing that they don't care at all."

"You're right. Being in the upper echelons is not the respected profession it used to be, but it's that way with everything these days, Jules. Nurses don't get the credit that doctors do, even though they do sometimes so much more. They just don't have the training and the respect. We have plumbers and electricians doing great work for large companies, but it's the company that gets the glory for it. We all know that. I remember the advice you gave me. 'Search your heart and make sure it's what you really want to do.' And if you want to do it, I'll support you 100%."

Julie was so grateful for Luke's support, although it made her nervous. The decision was hers to make, right or wrong. There would be no one else to blame. It was going to fall squarely on her shoulders. She sat back in her seat and pondered his comments.

She was pleased they'd bought the Sprinter van, although it did tighten their finances. It was perfect for taking the girls camping. It wasn't a four-wheel drive vehicle, so it rode very nicely on a Mercedes Chassis, a very smooth ride with leather heated seats and all the bells and whistles. They'd bought it used so they had only paid about half of the original sticker price.

Usually at gas ups and rest stops, Julie would get out sandwiches and get cold drinks out of the refrigerator, but they tried not to use the van's restroom and shower except for emergencies. That way it was easy maintenance; they didn't have to worry about draining tanks, the level of their gray water or black water or fresh water, and they could just drive. She and Luke often took turns being the driver so they could make great time getting to places without having to stay overnight. One could drive while the other slept, and the girls had the bed in back.

If they needed a longer rest on trips, there was always a chain of restaurants and big stores that allowed overnight or temporary non-hookup campers. So as long as they stayed to the main highways, the routes were direct and simple. They saw a lot of beautiful countryside, and it was the cheapest way for all four of them to travel.

They stopped at a local truck stop to gas up the U-Haul, and Luke topped off the Sprinter. She accompanied the girls to the women's restroom, always wary of strangers in these roadside rest stops. But this one was clean and nicely shaded, and this time of year in the early fall, the traffic was fairly light.

She set up sandwiches and waters at a picnic table nearby, and all of them sat together, the adults mostly listening to the girls banter back and forth, and just enjoyed the day. She was grateful she was safe, and they were coming home. She missed her own house most of all.

"We're going to show you the beach that's really close to our house. I mean, it's like ten blocks away, not far at all," Amy said. "You have to go with an adult, but it's really a nice walk. The beach is beautiful too. Did you ever go to the beach up north at your old place?" she asked.

Maron was the first to answer. "Oh, the beaches up north are terrible. I mean, you have to wear a wetsuit just to get your feet wet. It's so cold. Lots of rocks and windy. I don't like it. I like going to the country and going skiing. Are you close to skiing?" she asked.

Amy and Jessica stared at their mom, looking for an answer. Julie was glad to help them out.

"We're about the same distance you are to skiing in the Sierras. We haven't really taken that up much. With the beaches so nice, we hang out there. And we get together a lot with the other SEAL families. We have backyard parties and bonfires quite often. They're looking forward to meeting you, and I think you're going to love it there. It's a whole new lifestyle, though, I'll be honest with you."

Maron shrugged and attended to her sandwich.

"I love the beach," said Lindsey. "Grandma and Grandpa took us one time when they went to Santa Cruz, and we loved it. We loved it so much we all asked Mom and Dad if we could move there."

She covered her mouth quickly at the mention of her parents. Her eyes searched from side to side but didn't focus on anyone in particular. Julie reached across the table and took her other hand in hers.

"Lindsey, it's all right. I don't think that's a bad thing to talk about at all. You're going to have lots of really happy memories. And I want to hear them all.

It's going to be new for me. So don't worry about what you share, okay?"

Julie could see that Lindsey was about ready to erupt into a sobbing session, but instead of doing so, she nodded her head and held her breath, staring down. Amy leaned her head into Lindsey's shoulder and comforted her.

"It's okay, Lindsey. We love you so much, and we are so excited to show you everything we love about San Diego. And of course, we're close to all those water parks and Disneyland."

Kiley immediately erupted. "Disneyland! Oh, please, could we go there soon? Please?"

Luke nodded. "I think we can arrange that. Weather's nice, and school's in session so it's probably a pretty good time to go. We'll do that soon. That's a promise."

A cheer erupted from the little crowd in front of the adults. Julie breathed a sigh of relief at the realization they had just skirted the sad subject of the loss of their parents. She hoped that, in the future, it would get easier and easier.

But today, sitting next to her husband and watching her five children, today was a good day.

THEY ARRIVED AT their home in Coronado well after dark. The girls were fast asleep, huddled together in the queen-sized pull-out bed the couch made at the rear of their van.

"Let me get upstairs and arrange things a bit," she said to Luke.

"Let me know if you need help."

"Once I get the girls inside, you and Nick can go over to the warehouse, if you want."

He gave her a nasty look. "Tonight? You really mean that?"

She realized her comment had not been thoroughly vetted. Of course they were tired. Nick especially would be after having been jostled around in the U-Haul smelling of gasoline. "Sorry. I'll set something out for Nick on the living room couch, and you guys can do it tomorrow."

Luke bowed. "Thank you, ma'am," he whispered, feigning tipping his cowboy hat that didn't exist.

She tore upstairs, put the twin beds in Amy's room together, and added another pillow and an extra blanket. Then she went into Jessica's room with the bunk beds, straightened the sheets, and brought out another pillow and a thick comforter in case someone decided to sleep on the floor by themselves. She was going to let them choose tonight, and then they'd sort out a longer-term solution tomorrow.

The girls were rubbing their eyes, exiting the van. Jessica had her teddy bear under her arm and was holding hands with Kiley. The two of them ran inside. Julie heard Jess's excited instructions, ending with, "I've got bunk beds too!"

Maron followed behind them, and then Lindsey and Amy were next.

"Amy, why don't you show Maron and Lindsey your room while I get some soup going in the kitchen? We'll have a light snack, and then it's bedtime."

With the girls safely inside, Julie walked over to Nick and gave him a hug.

"Thanks so much for your help."

"No problem, Julie. You guys would do the same for us." He stretched his back, Julie hearing a loud pop as his spine adjusted.

"Ouch!" Luke barked.

"You think jumping out of planes is hard. Try working in the field all day or replanting lavender. I don't think I've sat so long in years. But those were mighty nice sandwiches, Julie."

"Oh, that was all Mom. And the cookies are Dad's favorite."

Luke wrapped his arm around her waist and drew her into him. "I'll lock up. Nick, you go inside. You smell like you need a shower."

"If only to get rid of the gasoline smell. A few more hours of that, and I'd be puking my guts out."

"I've got you set up on the couch and laid out some

fresh towels," Julie directed.

Several minutes later, all eight of them were sipping warm tomato soup and munching on some carrots and celery they had in the refrigerator. Julie noted both Luke and Nick appeared tired.

She knew her parents would be worried they made it home safe, so she called them up with FaceTime so they could see all five of their grandchildren. After trying to control the phone, she finally just gave it over and let the girls tell their excited tales about the trip. They did what Julie and Luke could never do: reassure them that all was well. At least for now.

Luke was smiling warmly at her. He gave her a thumbs-up. But Julie could see he was dead tired.

The girls' conversation was degenerating, and after one of the girls accused another of having potty mouth, she confiscated the phone and graciously signed off, blowing her parents a big kiss. Luke was in the background with, "Bye, Mom and Dad. Love you."

She set the phone down. The boisterous, simple dinner was going to be a regular thing, she realized. It came with the territory. She wanted them to feel safe in their new home.

Luke looked like he was about to fall asleep in his bowl.

"Go on, you two. Get yourselves to bed. I can finish up and get them tucked in."

"No, I'll help," Luke insisted.

"Mister, get your butt upstairs, and you take that shower. No arguments!"

The girls giggled, excused themselves, and followed their dad to the second floor. Julie turned to Nick. "Again, I know I've said it before, but thank you."

"I'm good. The timing was okay. Another week and we'd have been too busy. Our next event isn't for another ten days, and Devon's got that so organized, it practically runs itself."

"She'll have to give me some pointers, then," Julie said as she brought the dishes into the kitchen. Nick helped her carry what she couldn't.

"You being a teacher, you'll do fine."

"Well, it's one thing to manage twenty-five precocious second graders and completely another to manage and care for five daughters, ages all within four years of each other, and three of them having just lost their parents. I have a lot of catching up to do. I have to learn their routines, their preferences. I want them to feel welcomed here."

"I thought Luke was going to stay home and take care of everything."

She stared at Nick as she slammed the dishwasher shut. "Are you mad? Have you ever known a man to be able to handle that, I mean really handle that? There's an old saying about two parents who work. Only the mother knows their shoe sizes, and she's always the one the school calls if there's a problem."

"Better not tell Luke you feel that way."

"No. Bless his heart. Luke will try his best. I'm not worried about that. Not worried about the girls either. I'm worried about Luke."

CHAPTER 7

J ULIE WAS UP and out of the house by seven in the morning, which meant breakfast, showers, breakfast cleanup, and unloading all the boxes were going to be Luke's job for the day. That and, of course, caring for five little girls, ages six to ten.

Nick laughed at him several times when he came out to the dining room with a frying pan in one hand and a spatula in the other, wearing one of Julie's flowered aprons—and none of the girls paid any attention to him.

"Honest to God, Luke, I think you're crazy. Just batshit crazy."

"We try to watch our language when we have little ears listening, Mr. Dunn," Luke said, imitating a Mrs. Doubtfire-type character.

"My apologies."

Luke swirled his spatula in the direction of the girls as if it was a fairy godmother's wand. "And as you can see, they were not paying any attention to you, either. So there you go."

"You're used to getting things done, Luke. If somebody doesn't do something, you're used to yelling at them, shouting, demanding they finish the job. Think of all the times you've had to do things to restore someone's life or keep them from bleeding out. You weren't nice about it, and nobody expected you to be. Now, all of a sudden, you're gonna be Mr. Happy House-husband?"

Luke walked over to him, irritated all the way down to his athlete's foot crusting his little toe on the right side. He whispered to his friend, "That kind of talk is going to get you no breakfast and a quick boot from the house. You stop that, Nick. I'm not going to have it, you hear?"

"I got you. But if you boot me out of the house, who's going to help you unload that truck?"

"I have it on good authority that we have some gentleman SEALS on their way over to do just that. Not only that, but I've got a couple gorgeous SEAL ladies coming over to help watch the kids so we can complete that. So you see, it's all under control. All of it was arranged last night before I went to bed, and God bless Christy, she's coming through for us. You know how she takes care of Kyle's team."

Nick nodded. "Indeed, I do. She's one of a kind,

just like Kyle is."

"I don't know who he is sending, and I don't think it'll be him because he said he had meetings today. But we're supposed to have five guys. I think it'll only take us about an hour to get this junk offloaded."

"Did you ask Julie about the pink boxes?"

"No, I was going to bring one home tonight and see what she wanted to do with it. I was going to ask for suggestions." Luke wiggled his eyebrows up and down, waving his greasy magic wand in front of Nick's face. He turned and headed back to the kitchen, still gripping the empty frying pan with his left hand.

"Okay, who wants another egg?" he asked the Peanut Gallery.

"I want French toast," said Lindsey.

"I want pancakes and bacon," said Kiley.

"Daddy, can we have smoothies too?" asked Jessica.

With a sigh, Luke threw the frying pan and the spatula into the kitchen sink and walked to the head of the table with his hands on his hips. He knew Nick was going to have a hard time keeping it all together, because he knew how ridiculous he looked in this flowered apron. But he was trying to keep it light and fun. He figured they would cooperate better if they were having fun.

"Look, you guys. I am not a professional cook. I am not your maid, and I am not your butler or the housekeeper. I am a sometimes cook, and I can cook breakfast, but only one kind of breakfast. We're not going to be making these orders for five or six entrees for all these meals, okay? Just want to make sure you understand that."

"Okay," most of the girls said.

"I don't eat bacon. I'm a vegetarian," said Maron.

"Good to know then. Do you eat veggie burgers or veggie bacon?" he asked her.

"I like veggie burgers, but it has to be on multigrain buns, and I might be lactose intolerant, so I have to have the vegetarian cheese."

"Well, I've never bought vegetarian cheese or butter, and I think we can find some whole grain bread, but, Maron, you're going to have to give me a break here, because we don't eat that way."

He realized too late he had probably come across too strong. Maron's lower lip began to pucker and protrude. Tears streamed down her cheeks.

Damn it. Got to be careful, Luke, he said to himself.

Her crying stopped.

"Look, Maron, you and I will have a special shopping day, okay? We'll go to the store, and you can show me some of the things that you like to eat and can eat, okay?"

She looked up at him meekly. Now he understood why she was so skinny. In Luke's opinion, anyone who was a vegetarian was starving himself and would die before the age of forty. But that was a conversation and an argument for another day. He was encouraged by her attempt at smiling.

"Okay. Can we go today?"

If Maron was a new recruit or a young medic trainee under Luke, he would've dished out a healthy dose of "don't try to fuck with me." But this was Maron, and she was nine years old, a vegetarian, and had just lost her parents. Luke knew he was not going to win that battle, and Maron knew it too. That's why she pushed the envelope. He realized that was probably one of her skills.

Everybody has skills. He thought her skillset was irritating the fuck out of grownups. And he had to admit, the world needed people like that occasionally. But right now, he was hoping he could turn her personality around a little bit, perhaps soften it. And she was probably reacting to all the negativity that had befallen her. Of course, she was going to take it out on the big old tatted bad guy wearing a flowered apron. So be it. He was up for the task.

He walked over to her, patted her back, and then knelt so that they were eye to eye. "I have a lot of things to do today. First of all, I have to unload all the boxes we brought down from Santa Rosa. I have men showing up to help me with that. We have a few other things

I have to do related to your parents' estate then a meeting Julie and I have to go to this evening. I promise you, before the end of tomorrow, I will take you shopping. And you can pick out anything you want to eat, within reason."

That brought a wide grin on Maron's face, and Luke was finally satisfied he could please her. If it had been appropriate, he would've grabbed her and given her a big hug.

Of course, raising five girls meant no good moment was going to last all that long. Amy asked him if she could go shopping too and pick out some of the foods she liked to eat. Jessica agreed, thought it was a good idea. And so Lindsey and Kiley were all for it too. Before he knew it, he was going to have five little girls wheeling him around in this supermarket, possibly spending a week's pay on items they usually didn't carry. But this was day one, and if it made them happy, he was glad to do it.

"All right, I can see defeat when it stares me in the face. We'll try to get it in tomorrow. I don't think today's going to work."

He cleared the table and sent them up to the room to finish unpacking and, those that hadn't, to get a shower and brush their teeth. Maron held back, hesitant to go upstairs.

Luke looked over at Nicholas who was chuckling

already, trying not to spill his coffee. Maron slowly walked over to him.

"Yes, Dear?"

"I don't like sleeping on the floor."

"Okay, so you slept in Jessica's room? In the bunk bedroom, right?"

Maron nodded.

"So tonight you should sleep with Lindsey and Amy. There's plenty of room for you there."

"All three of us in the same bed?" Her little devilish face did irritate him, and it was going to soon be time for him to start setting some boundaries and limits to how much he was going to take. But it wasn't time yet for that.

Very carefully, Luke explained, "We will make sure that those arrangements are all handled tonight or tomorrow. If we have to buy more furniture, more beds, we will. But right now, you know we weren't set up for this. I'm just going to ask you, Maron, if you just give it a chance. Three to a bed, especially at the size and the ages you guys are, is no big deal. There's more than enough room for all three of you, and if you don't like it, then you can sleep on the floor in Jessica's room."

"Why can't Jessica and Kiley sleep in one bunk bed and I sleep in the other one? I want the top one."

"Maron, let's not do this. I'm asking everybody to

be flexible. We're being flexible too. Please, just try to fit in."

Luke could tell immediately Maron wasn't the type of child to do that. She was going to be testing his limits right and left until he caved or until he reacted inappropriately and got in trouble. He'd seen it happen with other kids. His Amy and Jessica never behaved that way, but he'd seen other kids set their little brothers and sisters up until they blew it, overreacted, and then they were the ones punished. He could see Maron was very skilled at manipulating adults and children. And she wasn't afraid.

"We're going to do things my and Julie's way here. And you can tell us as much as you like what you would prefer, and if we can, we'll accommodate you. But if we can't, you're going to have to accept that. Life isn't perfect, as you already know."

Maron looked up at his face, fear written all over her.

"I'm sorry. That was unkind. What I mean is, we can't always get what we want." He was hearing the song playing in his brain while he was going crazy trying to tamp down his irritation, practicing patience, understanding, and the alternative to shouting and ordering and reacting.

"If I don't like it here, can I go home?"

"No, Sweetheart. This *is* your home. Now go on

upstairs, get your teeth brushed, comb your hair, and get ready for some new playmates."

She looked at him with a puzzled expression.

"I have a couple of ladies who are going to come over and bring their children with them. They're wives of other SEAL team members. They're going to babysit for a few hours until we get our work done. You're going to really enjoy them."

"Boys?" she said with a wrinkled nose.

He already knew Brandon Lansdowne was going to be one of them. He couldn't wait to see how Brandon would handle Maron. "Yes, dear. Boys will be coming over." It gave him great satisfaction to tell her that.

Brandon arrived with several other children, all brought by Tucker Hudson's wife, Brandy. They had been told the girls had a blow-up swimming pool in the backyard, so as soon as they walked in the front door, shoes were kicked off, shirts removed, towels were wrapped around their necks, and they headed for the backyard almost without greeting the adults. Luke went upstairs and told the girls to get their suits on and join the others outside. In total, there were now ten kids in the backyard, the oldest thirteen and the youngest five.

Most of the kids knew each other so well there was little argument and a lot of cooperation. Luke had always noted that during those family parties and get-togethers on the beach. The kids probably inherited this from the way their parents treated each other, primarily the men, but most of the women as well. It was a culture, he realized. And as he saw this younger generation playing, talking, splashing, and teasing, none of them displayed bullying and meanness. They were well cared for, monitored closely by Moms and Dads and knew how to behave. Not that they were perfect, of course.

Luke remembered when he sat in on the preschool visit with Kyle and Christy, when Brandon was caught swearing and being belligerent with another child at the school. The teacher had threatened he'd be expelled, and Kyle was nearly beside himself. Brandon, now a lanky boy of twelve or thirteen, was beginning to spurt up in height and was taking on a leadership role amongst the kids. Although he was not always the oldest, he usually did a pretty good job of making sure the little ones were taken care of. Luke admired his athleticism and his respect for human life. He knew that came straight from Kyle and Christy.

Shortly after Brandy and Luci Begay arrived, several other team guys and former team guys showed up in a four-door Hummer. Danny was there. So was Jameson Daniels, Tucker Hudson, and two other prospects or tadpoles, as they called them, new guys to the team who hadn't been on a deployment yet. They rode over to the warehouse together, some in the cab of the U-Haul and some in the Hummer. Luke registered the load with the gentleman at the front desk at the mini warehouse complex. He was given keys after he paid the deposit and six-month storage fee and was shown where to take the van. It was a well-lit storage facility, although not in a necessarily good neighborhood, but it was locked and monitored with security cameras. The gates were only open during daylight hours, which was done to thwart any kind of criminal activity so common to some of the other complexes in San Diego. A big arms bust had occurred at one several years ago, with several regular Navy guys and a couple of Marones purchasing guns and ammo from detaching sailors and selling them on the black market to gang members desperate to get their hands on them. There were nearly twenty who got booted, including one SEAL who lost his Trident. Several of them were now serving time in jail.

They made short work of the boxes, stacking everything as it was labeled, making sure to keep the crystal on top of the stacks so they wouldn't get crushed. There were several comments made about the pink boxes, and Luke was tired of explaining what they were, so he just clammed up and asked them to keep going. However, at the end, he had Nicholas put one of the boxes back in the U-Haul.

"What's that for?" he asked Luke.

"I told you, remember? It's going to be an experiment. I want to show Julie. We'll see what happens."

"Man, you're way more daring than I'd be. Does she even know about this stuff?"

"I kind of mentioned it to her, but I don't think she paid attention. It was hard for me to believe. Anyway, we'll just have some fun. I'll joke around with it. I mainly want her to tell me what she wants me to do with it. I couldn't very well leave it in their garage, could we?"

"Nope, well, that's a story I'd like to hear."

The guys who arrived in the Hummer said their goodbyes, and he thanked them for their hour and a half service. "I owe you a good dinner. I'll make it a steak dinner too."

Several of the team guys gave him a manly hug and whispered things privately. Mostly, everyone said they had his back, they knew he was not going to be on the next deployment or two, and they hoped he'd be joining them again soon. They all asked to be remembered to Julie, and some of them knew the Christensens and asked to be remembered to them as well.

"You drew a bad card there, Luke. But I can see you're going to make this work," Danny Begay said. "Bending families together, we found out how hard it was when we adopted Ali, but you know what? It was the best thing that ever happened to our little family. Your heart gets bigger when you can take care of someone else's child. There's no greater joy in the world. And these girls need you. I'm glad you can be there for them."

"Thanks, Man. I really appreciate that, Danny. I appreciate all you guys. I may not be with you on deployment, but I'll be with you in spirit. My heart's always going to be with you guys. So you better come back, okay?"

Everyone chuckled, said their goodbyes, as Luke and Nick locked up, exited the storage facility, and headed back to Coronado.

"So you're going to stay over one more night or what are your plans, Nick?"

"I was going to hop on a plane, but I didn't make any reservations. I think Jameson's got a little gig going at one of the clubs. I thought I'd pop over there if I can borrow one of your cars."

"No problem. We'll get this puppy taken back, and then I'll return it to the yard tomorrow. If you could help me with that, that would free up Julie for work."

"Sure thing." A couple of seconds later, Nick added, "Can I take your camper van?"

"No late nights, just in case we have to take the harem some place in an emergency, okay?"

"I'll be home by ten, Dad."

Brandy and Luci were still overseeing the huge water fight absorbing the entire backyard and part of the neighbors. Luke had invested not in water guns but water cannons that could shoot fifty feet or more when properly filled. They enjoyed watching the war play out in front of them.

Nick used the downstairs bathroom to take a shower and get ready to see Jameson perform. He told Luke he promised Jameson they'd meet for a bite beforehand.

While in the shower, Luke got a call from a highway patrol investigator, who was looking for Julie.

"She should be home within the hour. Can I take a message? I'm her husband."

"I'm going to have to talk to her as well, but you can relay the information. We have ruled out accidental and mechanical trouble as the cause of the crash that killed your sister and brother-in-law."

Luke swallowed hard.

"We now believe it was an intentional act."

CHAPTER 8

JULIE WAS EXHAUSTED from her day at the office. She'd had more meetings about issues than time to help straighten out the issues themselves. There were reports due, her input was needed for the budget for next year, and she had several interviews on the phone, which were going to lead to future teacher hires. They also had several concerns about substitutes getting other jobs and not being available for the existing staff. One third grade teacher was going to be out the rest of the year on maternity leave and had requested a substitute who was approved by another school district but had never been approved in Julie's.

She'd had several inquiries from other principals as to her application for the superintendent's job, as Devin McNally was leaving at the end of the year, just before Christmas. Julie hadn't applied as of yet but intended to.

The private school system Julie's district was affiliated with was made up of thirty elementary-middle school combinations and four high schools, with a sports program that attracted great men and women athletes who had a chance to receive scholarship monies, based on family income.

The district stretched from the Los Angeles area all the way to the southern border. Although not all faith-based, some of the schools were and elected to join their system for the academic programs and scholarship potential. Their donor base was huge and generous. Each school had the ability to order specialized classes with approval of the school board, which governed the whole system, the parents in that school, and their respective principals, like Julie.

They even sponsored a home-schooling program, and students could flow inside and outside the physical schools upon approval, which worked very well during the pandemic. With the support of the school board, Julie's biggest collaboration was with the parent-teacher board she'd created and set up as an elected group of twelve. The district was impressed with this idea and wanted to implement it throughout their system, so her candidacy looked favorable.

At least that's what the buzz was. She didn't mind it one bit.

Parents had always been an important part of her effectiveness, unlike other principals who were often at a tug of war with them.

But the State of California exerted its power over even private schools more and more, sometimes requiring changes to their curriculum without notice and without sound implementation methods. And the educational goal definitions were very sketchy and not well-defined, therefore easy to unintentionally break, resulting in fines. It had gotten so contentious at times in other areas that the district had to hire their first lobbyist, who also worked for other networks of private institutions, both faith-based and not all over the country. He was based in California, however.

So far, no major problems had occurred. But it did tend to alter some of the creativity in their curriculum and methods, for fear of the "Big Bears," as the parent-teacher group called them, the administrators for the State of California and their teacher union reps that inserted themselves mercilessly on unprepared districts. Julie wanted to see to it that their excellent program flourished with as little interference as possible.

Sampson Biggs was one of the most power members of the governing school board. A former NFL star, he maintained a successful player representation firm, recruiting kids from the projects with a past like his was and giving them opportunities they wouldn't otherwise have. His job was to spot talent for the district to feed into the four high school athletic programs the public schools couldn't compete with.

He wandered into Julie's office at the end of the day.

"Got a minute?" he asked. Julie had been filing reports online and set aside her laptop, inviting him to sit in front of her at the desk.

"Sure. What can I do for you?"

Biggs almost didn't fit into the armed wooden chair he was offered.

"We've noticed you haven't applied for the superintendent's job. Is there some change in your plans? I heard about your brother and sister-in-law. I'm very sorry for your loss, Julie."

"Oh, thank you, Sampson. I appreciate that. Yes, it's been somewhat of a juggle, but we're getting adjusted. Luckily, Luke is between deployments, so he's been shouldering most of it. We've just began the process of blending my brother's kids into our household. So far, no blow-ups, no major problems. But I'd be lying if I told you it was easy."

"I can't imagine. Knowing you two, I'd say those kids are lucky. Boys? Girls?"

"Three girls. So now that makes five. Poor Luke was outnumbered before; now he's completely crushed."

They laughed at that.

"So are you going to be able to take on the new position if it were offered to you?"

"I'm still very interested. Frankly, it's just been a matter of having the time to do the application. I haven't had to write an essay on my thoughts of teaching, management, and curriculum for years now. I'd like to take my time and do a good job of it. Make the board's decision an easy one."

"That sounds promising. I'm glad to hear that."

"No worries, but I appreciate you checking up on me."

"Well," he said, standing, "I just wanted to stop by and let you know how sorry the entire board is with your family's loss and to reassure myself that this hasn't changed your trajectory. I know I've said it many times, but you are the one I want in that position. Don't take too long, okay? Until I get that application, I doubt I'll sleep."

Julie was flattered with the compliments, even felt her face flush.

"Thank you, Sampson. That's very kind of you to say. I appreciate your support a great deal. Means so much to me to be working where I'm wanted."

"I think it's an issue of trust. Your husband being a Navy SEAL, we appreciate what it takes to be married to an elite warrior like that. Sort of like being married to a professional athlete, as my wife reminds me and did all the time back in the day—I wouldn't deem to compare myself to the work your husband does and how it must affect your whole family. But failure isn't an option in the Paulsen household, is it?"

Julie chuckled as she took his extended hand in a firm shake.

"No, it's not. I have to remind Luke about that sometimes when I have to overrule him. Let's say that this new phase of our family life is humbling and giving him an opportunity to stretch and grow in ways he never knew he needed. But you're right, he's made it a mission, and he's determined to succeed."

Biggs nodded, pointing at her. "You're special, Julie. Don't keep me hanging."

As soon as he left, Julie sat back in her chair and breathed a sigh of relief. Forces all around her were pushing her to only one outcome: she needed to take the superintendent's job, if she could get it. And with Biggs' support, while there were no shoe-ins in life, really, it was about as close as it could be to one.

But she wasn't going to celebrate just yet. Luke's job was what she worried about most. She was confident he'd succeed being Mr. Mom and was grateful he'd be out of the killing fields for a few months, perhaps longer if he quit, but she knew Luke. She was worried about all the litter he'd create along the way. He was, after all, a human tornado: unpredictable, capable of upending things and altering everything around him. There was a cost-risk evaluation going on in her head she sometimes found troubling.

When she got home, she noticed Nick's pillow and blankets folded on the couch, indicating he was probably going to stay over another night. She called out for Luke, who responded from upstairs that he was reading to the girls.

She set her briefcase down in the study, plugged in her laptop and phone to charge, and took the long stairway up to the bedrooms, holding onto the handrail. She was hoping they could turn in early. With one good night's rest under her belt, she would probably start to get her energy back.

Inside Amy's room, all the girls were seated around Luke, who was reading them Alice in Wonderland. It had always been one of Julie's favorites. Little Jessica came over and greeted her. Luke stopped briefly with a, "Welcome home, Sweetheart," and then continued on with the book. She retired to the master bedroom, stripped off her clothes, and took a long, hot shower. She was in the process of putting on her nightie when Luke entered the room, closing the door behind him.

"Where's Nick?" she asked.

"He's taken the van. I said it was okay obviously. I hope you don't mind. Jameson's having a little gig over at Pierre's Bar & Grill. I don't think you've ever been there before."

"Yes, I have. We had a bachelorette party there one time."

"Ah, you are so right. I forgot about that. Well, he'll be back before ten, and I decided to let him use the van because the U-Haul truck is just huge and hard to park."

"No, that's fine. You'll take the truck back tomorrow? You got everything done?"

"Yup. Got it all loaded at the mini warehouse. Filled the whole space."

"How was your day otherwise?" She slipped under the covers after propping the pillows up, grabbing her book from the bedside table, and putting on her reading glasses.

Luke sat on the edge of the bed and hesitated just long enough that it got Julie's attention.

"What is it?"

"I got a call from a highway patrol crash investigator. They've determined that Steph and Colin's accident, if you will, wasn't really an accident after all. It was an intentional hit."

"How did they figure that after all this time? How come they didn't determine this at the time of the accident?"

"Well, I didn't realize this until this evening, but the driver of the truck that hit them took off, and they only just found him. The truck was not currently registered, and actually, it had been reported missing from a construction site in Las Vegas several years ago. Now they have this guy in custody, and he's claiming somebody paid him five hundred bucks to hit them."

"Who is this guy?"

"He's a nobody. No record. Worked odd jobs. Bigtime gambler and drinker, I guess. But they didn't have a chance to get him tested that night, so alcohol isn't listed as a contributing factor."

"Maybe he just used it as an excuse to try to get some leniency. I don't know that I believe that. Who would want to kill my brother and Steph?"

"I just don't know what to say, Julie. I was going to call some of our friends, maybe Detective Riverton here in San Diego, see if he had someone he could recommend, but he's on vacation for a few days. Maybe Armando's step-dad, Sergeant Mayfield. I need somebody with some law enforcement background to look into this and see what they're really doing."

"Stephanie and Colin didn't have a care in the world. They didn't have enemies. I doubt it was intentional. I mean, they're just not the type of people who would get involved in stuff like that."

"I know, I know. I've told myself that a hundred times over since I got the call. But I'd like to have someone investigate on our behalf, someone who has some background or at least knows who this highway patrol investigator is, in case he has an agenda of some kind. And he sounded perfectly legit to me, but I would be easily fooled."

"So could I. But on that score, I think you're a better judge of human nature than I would be. This so far afield for me I can't comprehend it. It just seems so impossible we're even having this discussion, Luke."

She set her book on the side table and leaned forward over her knees tucked under the sheets. "What does this mean, Luke?"

"Well, first, we have to find out who might have wanted to harm them or, worse, kill them."

"So you actually believe this dude?"

"I'm just checking out all the angles. You know me."

She smiled up at her handsome husband. "I do. I know you can't help it."

"No, it's a good thing, Julie. If it's plausible, and I don't know for sure whether or not it is, then we have to assess whether or not that leaves us and the kids exposed."

"You're worried that some of it would rub off on us?"

"We don't know, do we?"

"I prefer my pink bubble, the 'cone of deniability.'"

"That's why I just would feel a whole lot better if someone on the inside would get me some information. I need to know what they're investigating and who the players are. It sounds like it could be directed against either one of them. But I have a hard time thinking that a housewife and an architect would create enemies, do you?"

"You think they're investigating Steph and Colin?"

"That's what I need to find out."

"How could you possibly think some dark secret lurks there? Where do you get this, Luke?"

"It's my training. I don't trust anyone who wouldn't put down their life for me and my family."

"But couldn't this just be a rabbit hole? Maybe this isn't good for you, honey."

"That's why I need to know why the investigators are headed toward a murder investigation. That means there is a motive. We don't know what that is yet. Until we do, we have to suspect everyone, and that includes Colin and Steph."

"No, that's not consistent with who they are. Really strange. But you're right. Somebody who knows how things work and who can ask the right people the right questions, that's who we need. You called both Riverton and Detective Mayfield?" she asked.

"Yes, I left a message for both of them. I'm sure they'll get back to me as soon as they're available."

Julie noticed the pink box on the edge of the bed on Luke's side. "What's that?" she asked.

"Well, this is the other part of my suspicious mind working overtime."

"What is it?"

"Open it. It's from my sister's business. Did you

know anything about what she was selling?"

She began to crawl over the bed toward the box. "It was like home parties. I thought it was like cookware or knives or plasticware, something like that. She said she was doing these parties in ladies' homes in the area, and she was apparently pleased with herself. Now, I'm getting this from Mom, because Stephanie never told me what she was doing."

"Do you think they had some kind of a shadowy second life?" he asked her.

The question offended her first, and then she reconsidered her position. His delving into the possible sources of this information would help put it to bed and settle everyone's nerves, eliminate the stress of too many unanswered theories.

"I can honestly say that Colin and Stephanie were very much in love, and I mean Main Street Love, no question. They were an ideal couple and loved their girls. I never picked up any type of strange behavior, but what are you hinting at, Luke?"

"Do you think they were swingers?"

Julie laughed. "Oh God, no. That's the last thing in the world I would consider happening in their house. I mean, I'm sure they argued, but I never saw it. And they just seemed very compatible, very much in love. I don't see the need for any kind of a shadowy existence, some kind of an alternate reality. Is that what you're asking?"

"Well, look at this box, Julie. This apparently was

Stephanie's business. Selling what's in this box. I want you to look it over and tell me if this changes your opinion of them in any way."

She kneeled on the bed, hovering over the already-opened pink cardboard box. Inside, she was shocked to find the contents. There were all kinds of bright-colored gadgets, jars, tubes of creams, feathers, velvet handcuffs, laces, very skimpy underwear pieces, and vibrators of every shape, color, and size. She was completely speechless.

"We found this before our trip down here and just loaded it in the truck. I wasn't going to say anything, except for the sheer volume of boxes she had. I thought it was odd. But now, in light of this phone call I got, I'm wondering if there's some kind of a relationship between these two things. I mean, she kept this pretty quiet if this was in fact what she did on the side. I'm just wondering if she crossed the wrong people or if something happened, and it led to a misunderstanding, and somehow they got involved with some kind of nefarious group. I don't know. I just thought Stephanie would've told you or maybe Colin mentioned some-thing."

"No, I've heard nothing. And I really do think Colin would've told me if there was something going on. We never talked about their sex life, if this is what this is. It's possible one of them likes this stuff, and the other just went along, and they made a side hustle of it.

We know that she stopped the business and pulled down her website. I consider that kind of normal if you've all of a sudden decided you don't want to be involved in this. But Mom seemed to think she was doing quite well with her business and making a significant amount of money every month, which was helping to pay some of the school fees and camps for the girls. When she had decided to shut it down, Mom really didn't know why, because she assumed that Steph was quite happy with it. I'm almost positive Mom doesn't know about any of this," she said, pointing to the contents of the box.

"That's what I thought. I think we have to investigate further. I need somebody who has their finger on some of this kind of alternative behavior. On the surface, it looks fairly harmless. Just a bunch of colorful toys for party night between couples. I don't think there's anything wrong with that. Just a little experimentation. But the abrupt curtailing of her business and the accident that killed them coming under scrutiny just sets my antennas on fire. I can't just ignore it now. I have to find somebody who can help us get to the bottom line."

Julie reached into the box and picked out a pink penis-shaped vibrator, pressing a button. The vibrator buzzed, even lit up, started shaking in her hand, and then, as if waving goodbye, bent forward a few degrees before resuming the erect position again and stopped.

"Oh my. Luke. This is—is—"

"That wasn't the kind of investigation I was thinking of."

He took the vibrator from her hand, turned it off, and placed it back in the box. He picked up a little hand-held buzzer that fit over a person's middle finger.

He'd brought something like this home some years ago, and it had been fun, but over the years, they'd misplaced it. She knew what it was and how it made her feel, dammit.

"Appears to be a new model here. Maybe we could test a couple of these things?" Luke asked her.

She couldn't read his expression, except he focused on her lips. She felt her arousal, even though the timing of it sucked, was so inappropriate, was something she should easily purge from her thoughts, except it wasn't easy. Their sex life had suffered over the past few weeks, and she suddenly felt needy beyond desperate.

"Why, Luke Paulsen. I wouldn't know what to do with this stuff. I'm afraid you'd have to show me."

"That's exactly what I was thinking. It would be my pleasure, my dear wife."

CHAPTER 9

LUKE HAD ONE of the SEAL wives come over to watch the girls while he and Nick returned the U-Haul. Then he took Nick to the airport for the one-way trip home, and Luke paid for that ticket as well.

"You holler if you need anything, Luke. I wish I had more contacts with law enforcement, but if I run across anything, I'll let you know. After our run-in with the neighbor, we tend to stay away from the courts and law enforcement. We stick to weddings, the ranch, and making wine."

"You got it made, Nick. Again, thanks, and let us know if we can ever help you out as well."

"Be careful about volunteering. We might get you stomping grapes yet!"

Back at the house, Luke thanked Brandy and checked on the girls. He received a call from Gus Mayfield, the retired San Diego Police Sergeant, who had married Armando's mother. Indeed, Mayfield was family to the Teams, and many times guys would use him to obtain inside law enforcement advice and information. He was returning Luke's call.

"So what's going on, Luke?" His voice sounded even crustier than Luke had remembered.

"Sorry I had to be so cryptic, but I really didn't want to spell it out too much. I've got a situation with Julie's brother and my sister. You know about the accident?"

"Yes, we were all sorry to hear that, Son. How are you holding up?"

"Well, we've brought the girls here, and we're getting situated. We still have some trust things to deal with. But the biggest concern we have right now is the investigation into the crash."

"Oh? There's an investigation?"

"See, that's what I thought too. It's been a few weeks now, and nobody ever said anything about investigating it other than trying to locate the drunk driver who hit them. As it turns out, they've caught the guy, and now he's telling the investigators he was paid to broadside their car. And the truck was stolen, stolen off of a construction site in Las Vegas several years ago. Ownership of it is sketchy, and the guy who drove the truck is even more sketchy. I just don't have a good feeling about this, Gus, and I was wondering if you'd be willing to look into it for me. I know you still have contacts up in Sonoma County and the Peninsula."

"I do. I'm not sure what I can find out, but I can try certainly. Best to just let them do their job, though, Luke. It really isn't necessary that you get yourself involved in it."

"I know that's a good piece of advice, but it's more than that."

"How so?"

"Well, this is difficult to explain, but my sister had a mail order business—a side business, selling sex toys."

"Good Lord. That's a surprise. But I guess these days, I shouldn't be surprised at all. Still, I would never think Stephanie would do anything like that. And Colin? Boy, that's a big new one on me."

"We removed the boxes they had stored in their garage, with the house going on the market, and—"

"You're selling the house? You should keep it and make it into a rental."

"It's a huge, architecturally-designed house, Gus."

"Gotcha."

"We found a whole bunch of inventory, and frankly, I didn't think much of it, either, except that even Julie's mother didn't know exactly what the business was. We all assumed it was home fragrance or Tupperware or knives or something like that. She would have these parties at people's houses. I guess I can understand why Stephanie never said anything to me or Julie, so that part is okay, but she closed the business down abruptly right at the time they were coming back from a convention in Las Vegas. The timing of it, her closing the business and shutting down her bank accounts, is just odd. And then they have this accident and indications are that it was a paid-for hit. I mean, wouldn't you start to draw some conclusions there?" Luke asked.

"Well, the selling of the 'pleasure items' doesn't bother me. Hell, Felicia and I have been known to experiment a little bit, and I presume you and Julie are the same."

"I'm not saying a word. Not admitting anything. And I won't repeat that."

Gus Mayfield chuckled. "Well, a lot of things would surprise you. But we won't get into that. I do think it is worth looking into, and if you don't mind, I will do that and get back to you. Don't expect anything earth-shaking. They're going to strong arm me, and they're going to know I have a connection to the SEAL community down here. When they put it together, I don't expect they're going to open up their files to me or anything. But I would be cautious about who you tell about all this. Because the worst thing that can happen is something can get out there on social media and all of a sudden you got rumors. And rumors are really hard to combat. Let the police do their job unimpeded, and let's see what they come up with before you start disclosing anything to anyone else. And do not, whatever you do, talk to the media. Remember, the media is not your friend."

"That's sound advice, Gus. I've also called Clark Riverton, and I know he's headed-up several organized crime task forces here in San Diego. I'd heard he was getting ready to retire, but maybe he could look in different directions and help us out too."

"Well, I think he'd be more connected than I would certainly. Why do you think it's organized crime?"

"The Las Vegas connection. They were coming home from there when it happened."

"I see. Not sure it has much to do with it, but I'll do my best, and you can have Clark call me if he needs to. I'll share whatever I've got with him and with you guys. Now again, don't expect any miracles, because Felicia's got me doing all kinds of stuff to get ready for the holidays. Sometimes I think that's why she married me. She's planning to entertain her heart out here, and you know what she feels about her gardens, her flowers, and her house. So I don't think I can do this quick, but you let me know if you hear anything further in the meantime."

"Will do. Thanks so much."

The girls were outside in their swimsuits, nobody

in the pool yet, but sunning themselves in the warm early fall sun. Most of them were reading. Maron had fallen asleep on a chaise lounge. Luke figured he had about thirty minutes before he'd have to start putting together some things for lunch, so he went to his computer to research bunk beds. He found a site that sold double and queen-size bunk beds, which he calculated might fit in Jessica's room, but it wouldn't leave much room for anything else. He also found a Murphy bed/desk combination in another catalog that might work for Amy's room.

Knowing Maron seemed to like the bunk beds, he figured that would be the best way to go, so instead of checking with Julie first, he went ahead and paid for the bunk beds to be delivered to the house with a credit card. It was more money than he wanted to spend, but he hoped that the trust funds would be coming through soon and he'd be reimbursed. One thing for sure, it would handle a huge issue, and that was sleeping arrangements, which he knew would only get worse as the days went by.

He and Julie were supposed to meet with several teachers who were going to have the girls in their classes, and that was all scheduled for tomorrow. The following week, his girls and Steph's kids would be resuming their classes at school. The teachers had all been notified that everybody was taking a few days off, and nobody seemed to object to what they'd requested. It also gave Luke a chance to assess what interested the girls and to try to make them feel comfortable and at home.

He thought about Kyle's conversation with him about staying on the Teams or not and was grateful that he had the six months.

Luke decided he'd take the girls shopping, so he could check that one obligation off his list of things he had to do. He called them inside and promised them they could go out for fast food, providing they could find something that Maron could eat, and the girls were thrilled at the opportunity.

He loaded all five of the girls into the van and made his first stop at an organic grocery store, figuring Maron would have the best selection. But as they browsed the aisles, all of the girls jumping up to grab things and place them in the cart like a virtual smorgasbord, he discovered that Maron was the one who was picky, and his other girls were actually going to be filling the cart with very expensive items they really didn't need to get. And he didn't think they'd enjoy eating some of the things they picked, but he went along with it anyway. Maron was able to find her vegetarian cheese, vegetable spreads, organic peanut butter, and sugar-free jams, also the imitation bacon and garden burgers. She also liked to drink kefir and yogurt.

Luke felt like they were a small storm of activity when they got to the checkout counter. He got some amazing smiles and laughter as all five of the girls were talking at once, chattering amongst themselves, dashing in and out of the carts and playing tag. They knocked over a display of new cereals, sending boxes all over the floor. Several times, Luke had to step in and quell the chaos. He lost Jessica just as they were ready to leave the store and had to have her name announced over the loudspeaker. She'd gone to the bathroom but hadn't told anybody. That was another lesson and a long conversation that resulted in some tears.

As he pulled the cart out to the van, the girls swirling around him like a bunch of bees circling a beehive, he again had to remind them about situational awareness, watching for cars, watching for people watching them, all the things that he'd been trained and were second nature to him. His intent was to arm them with observations and techniques and talents that they didn't now possess. But the truth was, they barely listened to him, and that worried him no-end.

Next, they went to one of the local grocery stores, and Maron picked out several exotic fruits including dragon fruit, papayas, and organic bananas. He instructed her to keep them in a special green plastic bag, because the rest of the family was not going to eat organic. He bought several staples and the favorites of the girls, some frozen things that would make life easy for him, extra spaghetti sauce, and pre-made frozen meatballs for his Thursday night dinners, and other things. As he was meandering down the laundry section of the store, he got a call.

"Hey, Luke, I got an inquiry from somebody from San Jose, an investigative team."

It was Kyle, and the conversation surprised him.

"Wait a minute, somebody called you about me?" he asked.

"Yeah. Just asking questions about your background, whether you were a SEAL in good standing, how long you'd been there."

The girls boarded a long flat cart, and Lindsey started to push the others, heading around the corner.

"Just a minute, Kyle." He shouted, "Girls. You come right back here! Get off that d—that cart."

Sheepishly, they returned to him, hanging their heads. The long cart was abandoned in the center of the aisle and had to be moved by someone trying to approach from the other side.

"Hey, Kyle, sorry about that. I'm shopping."

"So that's what's going on. You're one brave son-ofabitch."

Luke sighed, both frustrated and beginning to feel exhaustion.

"Kyle, I just want to mention to you that we need to be careful about this. They're determining this was not an accident but that Colin and Stephanie were intentionally hit, as you know."

"Yeah, I know. Christy told me. I didn't give him much information. I just—"

"Who was this person who called you? Are you sure it was a police investigator?" he asked.

"Well, let's see. He gave his name as, let's see, Spencer Roberts. He's an investigator with... hmm, I didn't write it down or he didn't give it to me. I just thought he was from Highway Patrol or the Sheriff's office. Holy fuck, maybe he's a private investigator."

"That's what I mean. You see now?"

"I do."

"Well, I need to talk to Clark Riverton, and I've already talked to Gus Mayfield. I think we have to be very careful about answering questions until we figure out who we're actually talking to. With this turn of events, I don't trust anything that's going on."

"Okay, I got you. Damn it, Luke. I should have thought of this. I don't know why, I just thought it was going to help. I gave you a glowing recommendation. I said nothing about the troubles you've had in the past. I just answered his questions."

"What questions did he have?"

"Well, he actually asked if you had ever been involved in any altercations or fights on the Teams? If you'd ever exhibited behavior that wasn't up to the Navy standards. He also asked about Julie. And when that happened, I really clammed up. I probably should have before."

Luke didn't want to get angry with Kyle, but he knew the conversation was a total mistake.

"I think until further notice, Kyle, we ought to beg off any interviews unless they come to you in person. We're going to need to check their credentials first, and let me have Gus and Clark look into things first. And then we'll kind of know where we're at. But right now, I need you to be very quiet and very tightlipped. I know we're supposed to be honest, but you know when it comes to missions, we don't tell everybody what we're doing. And this is sort of turning into something like that."

"Are you sure it's not your imagination, Son? I mean, are you really sure?"

"I don't have anything but my gut reaction to it all, and if I think these things are related, then I have to check it out before I change my mind about it. You and I both know we stay alive because we stay focused on everything going on around us. This could affect our family if it doesn't go well. I have nothing to hide, but I don't want to volunteer to give information to a possible future enemy."

After they unloaded the van, the girls went outside to eat their hamburgers. They were able to find Maron fish tacos at the same hamburger stand he bought meals for the other girls.

Clark Riverton gave him a call. "I understand from Gus you got a situation brewing?"

Luke was grateful for this experienced detective and his no-nonsense attitudes toward law enforcement. He was glad that Mayfield had made the connection.

"Yeah, it's getting pretty crazy, Clark. I would appreciate it if you could come over and talk to Julie and me about this. Would that be possible?"

"Sure. What time does she come home?"

"Well, I assume you're back from your vacation—"

"Yeah, it was actually a seminar. Daisy went to a tattoo convention."

Clark had married the tattoo artist that most of the SEALS went to for their skulls and Celtic crosses and bands of barbed wire. Her studio had been left to her by the prior owner who had been taking care of SEAL Teams for twenty years and was a former SEAL himself before he passed away.

"I think about 5:00, 5:30 would work."

"I got it. I'll see you at 5:30, and if Julie gets delayed, no problem. I don't have plans for the rest of the evening."

Luke sighed, glad the team he was assembling was maybe going to help them stay out of trouble or, at the worst, get them some much-needed information. Watching the precious girls climb in and out of the pool, laughing and spraying each other with the hose, he wanted them to never know some of the deep, dark things of this world, some of the evil he was battling. And he knew evil existed everywhere. Even when you least expected it.

This new revelation about Steph and Colin had proved that, beyond a shadow of a doubt.

CHAPTER 10

W HEN JULIE RETURNED home, Clark Riverton's car was parked in the driveway. He and Luke were having a conversation in the living room. The girls were still having a water fight in the backyard, and at times, the hose sprayed the picture window in the dining room. Julie was upset that Luke had not been paying close attention. Their screams were echoing all around the neighborhood.

"Nice to see you, Julie. I'm Clark Riverton." He extended his hand. "I'm semi-retired, in charge of the violent crime task force here in San Diego County. Luke has asked me to come over and give you some advice and shed some light on what has gone on so far."

Annoyed, Julie spoke quickly, one eye on the mayhem in the backyard.

"That's fine, but—" She gave a stern look at Luke. "You're not paying attention to the girls. Do you know that kids and adults can drown in three inches of water? These girls are out there totally unsupervised."

Luke got up, quickly checked out the window, and turned back to her. She could tell he was going to disagree with her and wasn't happy with her criticism.

"Julie, I've been watching them all day. I took those fucking girls to the store, I bought a ton of specialty food, I've been cooking for them, and I've been cleaning the fucking house until my hands are sore and raw. I've been working my ass off. I can't even take a nap because there's nobody here to watch them, and—"

"Whose fault is that?" she asked him.

"Whoa, whoa, whoa, whoa. Hey, folks," Riverton started. "I don't want to intrude on anybody's feelings here, but I don't think this is a good time. I'll come back later, on another day."

"No. You stay right here," both Julie and Luke said in unison.

Julie raised one additional question to her husband.

"And I thought we were supposed to go down to the school tonight or did you forget about that, Luke?"

He was getting more irritated. Still standing, with his hands on his hips, he barked back at her, "I rescheduled it for tomorrow. You said it was going to be hard for you to make it tonight, so I rescheduled it, and instead, we're meeting with Detective Riverton. Don't you think that's a higher priority?"

Just then, they both heard somebody screaming in the backyard. Someone was in pain. Julie, of course, thought the worst.

"Goddamn it," she cursed as she raced through the living room and out through the kitchen door onto the patio. Luke and Riverton were left behind and had no time to respond before she was outside. All kinds of horrible thoughts went through her mind as she searched the yard and the patio and the pool and discovered that Amy had fallen down and skinned her knee, red blood flowing all over the place. She mumbled under her breath, "Where's a fucking medic when you need one?"

She looked up at the living room window and screamed, "Luke, get out here and bring your kit." Her peripheral vision noted the other four girls jumped and retreated to the edge of the lawn, away from her.

That started in motion the rumbling of the old house, as it shook. Even the windows rattled. That told her Luke had sprung to action, was opening the cabinet and bringing out his big medic bag halfway slung on his back. He ran to where Julie was and took a look at Amy's bloody knee.

Julie was trying to help her into the patio chair.

"Don't touch her, Julie. Leave her right there until I check out her bones." Luke's voice was sharp, rough, and cutting.

"She hasn't broken her legs. She just skinned her knee, can't you tell?"

"I don't make things up, Julie, I deal with certainties. And if she broke a bone, it could be worsened by making her stand up on it to sit in a chair. If you want her to sit in a chair, I'll put her there."

And that's exactly what he did. He picked her up and sat her in the chair.

Julie saw the other four girls suddenly go quiet, sitting together on the lawn in the shade, watching the fiasco of their parents argue over a minor wound. At least Julie thought it was a minor wound.

Luke felt from her hip down to her knee and then from her knee down to her ankle, squeezing and asking Amy if it hurt. He moved her ankle then raised and lowered her whole leg outstretched. When he moved the knee back and forth, she winced and complained.

"Ouch. Daddy, that hurts."

He touched and moved her joint carefully, getting his daughter's blood all over his hands as he did so. He dabbed the wound with some gauze from the kit and pointed to the scraped skin that had been bleeding.

Everything was negative, and Julie was relieved.

"Okay, so I'm going to clean this. You stay right here. I'm going to get some towels."

Amy started to cry. "I'm sorry, Mom. Why does he have to be such a terrible dad when he gets like this? I get afraid of him."

"I know, Sweetie. He doesn't mean it. He loves you. He gets worried. So do I."

"I didn't *mean* to fall. I was trying not to, but Maron tripped me."

Maron stood up and pointed back at Amy, "I did not. Amy's just so clumsy she doesn't know how to do anything without help. You slipped and fell because you weren't paying attention, Stupid."

"That's enough from all of you!" came the booming voice of her husband. "I have had just about enough with you guys. I have given you everything you wanted to do today, right?"

Nobody said a thing. Luke stood there with a dripping tea towel in his right hand.

"I said, haven't we done everything you requested to do today? I took you shopping, we went out for lunch, and you're getting to play in the swimming pool. I mean, you have a perfect life here. Be grateful for Chrissake, instead of a bunch spoiled brats."

Julie looked up at him. "Stop it, Luke. You're being an asshole."

Jessica inhaled and put her hands over her mouth. "Mother!"

"Well, I can see I'm not the only one who loses it. You know full well what it's like to take care of this group all day, and today is just… I've had it. I've had all kinds of unexpected crises, and we're trying to just have a normal life. This is a normal life, right? Is it going to be like this every single day?"

"I'm sorry. Maybe it's the apron, Luke. But I think the girls think you look ridiculous. They aren't obeying you, following your rules. You have to change."

Luke looked down at himself as if he'd forgotten that he was even wearing an apron. He quickly removed it and threw it on the ground.

"Fine. I'll get my own fucking apron."

"Luke? What's gotten into you?" In the background were four little girls with their hands over their mouth, Jessica with her palms over both ears, and all of them looking shocked and afraid.

"It's okay, Daddy," said Amy. "I understand. I'm the one who slipped and fell. I'm the one that caused all of this." She started to cry. "I'm so sorry, and I really didn't mean to ruin your day. And I'm sorry it's so hard for you to take care of us."

Her husband acted like he'd just been shot through the heart with an arrow. They heard the back door open and saw Clark Riverton's figure on the patio.

"Hey, guys, I'm going to come back another time."

Amy looked up at both her parents. "Who's he?"

"He's going to help us with something, Amy," said Luke. "Clark, it's not serious. We'll be done in just a couple of minutes. They're going to have a timeout, and I think we'll be able to finish our conversation. Don't go, please, because I honestly don't know when we're going to have the time to fit it in again."

"You're still being an asshole, Luke," Julie couldn't help whispering.

Amy looked at her mother. "I don't like it when you use Dad's words."

Of course they are dad's words. They certainly aren't mine, but I've been learning these ten years.

That almost got her laughing. Her husband did start to laugh. He chuckled all during the cleanup process, as he carefully put soapy water over the wound, picked out pieces of dirt and a leaf, rinsed it with clean sterile solution, and then applied some first aid cream over the raw skin. He then applied a three-inch gauze pad that had adhesive around the edges, making sure it was loose enough so it wouldn't pop off when she bent her knee.

"Your mother has a very ridiculously wicked mouth, Amy. But I still love her," he said as he leaned over and gave her a kiss on her cheek.

She was going to back away, but she accepted the small consolation. Her insides began to melt as he stared back at her with those blue eyes of his.

The girls were allowed to come into the family room, wrapped in their towels, keeping their bathing suits on for a later trip outside. Luke put on an

Avengers movie, and they all sat on the couch or the floor enmeshed in the action film.

Riverton looked like he was very uncomfortable and extremely out of place. But he kept his mouth shut and didn't offer to leave again, which Julie appreciated.

Julie addressed him as they walked back to the living room. "You know I always told myself that, when I had kids, I would never use the TV to occupy them. It's just not possible if you're trying to raise children these days. I mean, they do a good job entertaining themselves, but sometimes, you just got to turn something on that they can plug in to, and then they're preoccupied so they don't cause chaos. There are some days I had a hard time even concentrating on putting things in the dishwasher or emptying the laundry. And that was with just two. Now there are five."

"I'm beginning to learn some of those things myself. You get a routine going. It's not that bad. It's really not that hard," said Luke.

But Julie knew he had a new appreciation for all the years before she went back to teaching, when she stayed at home with the babies.

Julie put water on for coffee and asked Riverton if he wanted something else other than coffee.

"I'll have a glass of water. That sounds about perfect right now. I'm afraid, at my age, if I drink a cup of coffee I'm going to be up half the night."

"No problem." Julie got him a glass of ice water. She put her hand on Luke's shoulder, softening her tone toward him. "Honey? You want some water too?"

"Yes, please. Thanks." He grabbed her hand before she could remove it from his shoulder. Holding it to his mouth, he kissed her palm tenderly.

After the coffee was made and served, they settled in. Julie enjoyed the warm beverage and the half-and-half she put in it and asked the detective what his take was on their situation.

"Well, first of all, Julie, you need to know that we just started talking about it. So I don't even know all the facts of the case, although your husband has talked to Gus Mayfield, and Gus and I have discussed it a little bit. We really need to see what the background is of this guy who hit your brother and sister-in-law. We also want to see why they are giving a lot of weight to his testimony, saying that he was paid money to do it. It's just not normal. You don't take a big rig cab like that and T-bone a car. You could still be killed yourself. A car could explode. I mean, it's very dangerous to do. I just think, and I hope, he's just trying to cover up a DUI of some kind and using this ruse to try to get off or beat the charge. But I don't know."

"Did you tell him about the box of delights?" Julie asked Luke.

"You mean the Garden of Delights? The pink boxes?" he asked.

"You know what I mean." Hairs at the back of her neck began to stiffen.

"Clark, you wait right here. I'm going to go bring down the box to show you what my sister was doing in her spare time, and I'd like your opinion if you don't mind."

"No, I don't mind at all. I'm here to help any way I can."

While Luke was running upstairs and then back down again carrying the box, Riverton held his water glass up, "May I trouble you for some more, please?"

"Of course." She brought the pitcher of cold water from the refrigerator after filling his glass and set it on the table so he could help himself to more later on.

Luke brought a chair over from the dining room table and set the box on it, lifted the lid, and invited Riverton to look inside. "This is what we found, lots of boxes like these in Steph and Colin's garage. It appears she had a thriving mail order business selling these."

Riverton peered over the edge and began to chuckle.

"What's so funny?" Julie wondered.

"Pardon me, but if this doesn't look like the top drawer of my wife's bedroom vanity, I don't know what does."

Luke chuckled, but Julie wasn't amused. Luke immediately silenced.

"I think that falls into the category of TMI?" Julie said with a smirk.

"So I apologize. I'm probably dating myself, but we used to call these fuckerware parties back in the day. I guess they're still in style."

"You mean, this is a thing that's been happening for like years and years and years?" Julie asked him.

"Well, like anything, people are doing all sorts of home-based businesses to raise money these days, and lots of these cottage industry things are popping up all over the place. There's no harm in it. I'm looking at this stuff, and it's all pretty generic, pretty harmless stuff. It may not be the kind of thing that you guys would be interested in trying out, but—" He chuckled again. "You know, I think healthy couples probably can use some of this stuff. You know they say that, with all the crap going on in our society these days, people aren't getting it on as much as they used to."

"You view this as a sort of couple therapy enhancement. Is that what you're saying?" she asked him.

"No, Julie, they're toys, harmless toys. You ever wear a sexy nightgown for Luke? It's the same thing. Nothing wrong here. Nothing at all to worry about. And if it assuages your conscience about your brother and sister-in-law, I don't see how it harms anybody. They're just toys, and toys are not against the law.

Now, if we're talking about some heavy-duty S&M stuff where you have to have code words and handcuffs you can slip out of in an emergency, well, that's a whole other story, but this stuff is pretty tame. I've seen much worse. And I wouldn't be concerned, if that's what you're worried about."

"So you don't think this company with a base in Las Vegas, where they just came from attending a convention when they were hit, is related? You don't think that the fact that she was doing this on the side, they were in Las Vegas, and they get killed on their way home... you don't see any correlation with any of this?" Julie asked him.

"Not really," Riverton said. "You know, this isn't organized crime stuff. This is a little bit sexy stuff, I would call it." Riverton was squirming a bit in his seat.

"I think what Clark is saying, Julie, is he's familiar with this. And forgive me if I'm assuming too much, but you've probably used some of these items, right?"

"Well, it's a personal thing. You understand people have different kinds of tastes. I'm not condemning it, and I'm not admitting anything, but I will tell you, I wouldn't condemn anybody for playing around, experimenting. She probably had a good time selling this stuff. You know the women get together and have a couple glasses of wine. It sure would be a more interesting party than getting drunk and doing oil painting or selling cosmetics or plastic storage bins. Don't you think?"

"I don't know what I think. I'm just upset with the fact that they've called Luke and told him that this is a criminal investigation. That it was a deliberate effort on someone's part to hurt them. Maybe not kill them but definitely hurt them. And the fact that none of us knew anything about this before just adds credence to it. It's all a big mystery. We would be so grateful if you could look into their investigation and put our minds at ease."

"I got you. I'll do just that. But don't be expecting anything grand. I'm not going to be uncovering a counterfeit sex toys operation here."

Luke leaned forward and nodded his head and then mumbled, "Well, maybe you can do this one additional thing for us, Clark."

"What's that?"

"Do you know what we can do with twelve more boxes filled with shit like this?"

AFTER RIVERTON LEFT, they put the girls to bed. Luke told them about the bunkbed he'd ordered today and Maron especially was excited about having her own bed. She even agreed to sleep on the floor again.

Alone in their bedroom, Julie's phone rang downstairs.

"I'll get it for you," said Luke, who sprung to action, racing for the den, grabbed her phone, and handed it to her while it was still ringing.

"Oh good, It's Biggs. Probably something more about the superintendent's job I applied for." She took a deep breath before answering. "Hello, Sampson. How are you?"

Julie noted the edge to his voice that wasn't there when last they spoke.

"I'd like a short meeting with you tomorrow after you meet with the teachers, if you don't mind."

"Sure."

"Fine then."

"Um, not sure if you noticed, but I applied online for the superintendent's job."

"Yes, I saw that. We'll discuss it tomorrow."

"Is—is everything okay?"

"Have you watched the evening news?" he asked.

"No. Why? What have I not seen?"

"Just watch the news." Biggs hung up.

She stared at her phone. "That was very odd."

"Why did he call?" asked Luke.

"He wants to meet. I thought it was about the job, but now I don't know. Can you turn on the news, please?"

Luke did so. Both of them sat at the edge of their king-size bed and watched a report about how the fatal auto accident in San Jose some weeks ago was now being investigated as a murder-for-hire plot, and it involved a possible motive of financial gain. The reporter added that the murdered couple had been involved in a child pornography ring, possibly murdered to keep from cooperating with the police in Las Vegas who were trying to shut the ring down. A local San Diego family was also being investigated concerning this crime. More results would follow.

CHAPTER 11

"I'M GOING TO go to work today, Luke. I'm not going to let this media falsehood interfere with my job. There are teachers, students, and parents counting on me. I'm not going to fold and go run away."

She was her usual stubborn way when she was convinced she was right. Luke knew there wouldn't be any way he could talk her out of it, but he had to try—for her own safety and sanity, he had to try.

"But, Julie, think of it. You're going to be the subject of conversation all throughout the school district. It's not going to be hard for them to focus in on you. You've never had this kind of negative scrutiny, and eventually, the news media could start coming here. I think it's inevitable. I think we need to get an attorney and start doing some damage control."

"I just don't know where they're getting this information. And now the idea that some family member has killed them for their own financial gain? That's totally pure BS. If somebody did that, it couldn't be anyone from our family. There isn't anyone who would do such a thing. No, I have to act, walk, and conduct myself just as if I have nothing to hide, because I don't."

She could tell Luke all she wanted about how it was the right thing to go to work, but Luke was the one who slept next to her last night, and he'd be surprised if Julie even slept more than about ten or fifteen minutes without waking up in a cold sweat. He held her while she cried, he rubbed her back, he suggested she have some hot chocolate and brought it to her, he rubbed her feet, he placed lavender oil on her temples to help her sleep, and nothing seemed to work. But this morning, she was showered and dressed and ready to take on the day. Luke loved her tenacity and her stubbornness, but he was worried she was headed straight into a buzzsaw.

"Julie, if anything happens, and you feel like you're in the middle of a situation, you give me a call, and I'll be right over there."

She gave him a warm hug, opened the door, and faced the day.

He'd let the girls sleep in, and he made a couple of calls so that they could get coverage during their teacher meetings and Julie's meeting with Sampson

Biggs. Luke was going to insist he attend that meeting as well. There was no way he wanted her to be alone today.

He checked in with Kyle, giving him the update just in case he hadn't seen the news report.

"Yeah, I almost called you last night, but I thought, if you didn't see it, I'd let you guys sleep. But damn. Something's going on here, Luke. You got Mayfield and Riverton on this, don't you?"

"They're working on it."

"What do they say?"

"Yeah, I talked to Gus this morning. I guess Riverton's already called him. They're thinking of going up to Sonoma County or at least to the peninsula, to San Jose. There's a high-tech highway patrol investigation center in Campbell, which might be of help. But now they kind of have to be careful too, or they'll get somehow implicated. It's a very tricky thing, Kyle."

"Well, these guys know what they're getting into, Luke. You don't need to worry about them. The blue line still exists. God knows these guys in all departments have had to stick together. I say this in the positive sense of it, not what's on the news. There are rotten apples all over the country, but the good ones stay together and even try to get rid of the bad ones. Don't worry about them. You worry about Julie. I sure do."

"You know, I can't help but think how this is going to affect the superintendent's job. She was first in line for it, and now the guy who's the school board member handling the applications has called her in for a meeting. He did not sound his warm and fuzzy self like he was the other day, Julie said. I am not hopeful."

"Well, don't worry about it. It's all going to be revealed in time. Remember what you said. You two have nothing to hide. And you're sure about Steph and Colin?"

"God, I'd accuse Julie's mother if I ever got that far, Kyle. No way they've done anything wrong. It's just not like them. I know how they love their kids, children in general. I've seen it first-hand for years. Never in a million would I think that. I'm actually offended at the thought. It makes me sick."

Later, Brandy and one of the new Team guys' wives arrived in time so Luke could make the 2:00 appointment with the teachers at their school. He thought he'd done a good enough job cleaning the kitchen, but when Brandy walked in and saw what was left of his breakfast and then lunch preparations, she offered to finish.

"No, just spend your time with the kids. I can do this later," Luke said.

"I don't mind. I'm here to help. And the kids will be occupied. Besides, I have Peyton here. It'll only take me about ten, fifteen minutes. You go run along so you're not late. And I'll see you back what about 5:30, 6:00?"

"Yeah, I think so. I'll text you when we're on the way home."

"Good deal. Good luck."

Luke wondered what the new girl thought of his situation, since stories of Team family issues grew like wildfire between the members, primarily the wives. He was going to stop and make an explanation but just decided to let it ride. If Brandy felt they were involved in something nefarious, she wouldn't have come over and brought her kids. He had received lots of support from several phone calls earlier in the day, and Kyle had mentioned to him several times not to worry. He wished that he'd had an update from Clark Riverton or Gus Mayfield.

All in good time.

The school was filled to overflowing with activity. Children were being picked up, running down the hallways, bustling at a fast pace. The energy level in the place was amazing. He wished that growing up he'd had such a wonderful, vibrant place to attend school. He was so glad that his kids got the benefit of Julie's selection.

Julie was standing outside room 206, where they were to meet the first of three teachers. This was the second-grade teacher that was going to be taking Kiley.

Jessica was also in second grade, but might be in the other class. They needed to talk about this. He hadn't met the teacher before, Mrs. Pierce, but Julie said she was very good.

"Hi, Sweetheart. How's your day been so far?" he asked her.

She was non-committal and finally looked up at him. "I kind of lost my energy about an hour ago, to be honest. Tonight, I really have to get some sleep."

"I think you will tonight. Don't worry about anything. I'll make sure everybody gets to bed early, and you just turn in whenever you're finished, okay?"

"Thanks. The kids do cheer me up just being around them. I'm reminded that, even if this is hard, it's for them we're doing this. And the outcome we want isn't for us; it's for them."

"Just keep remembering that. It's good perspective. I feel the same way, Julie."

She slowly began another line of conversation, seeming hesitant to bring it up. "By the way, I'm sorry about our argument yesterday. I got to thinking about some of the things I said, and I want to apologize."

"It's been tough on both of us. We'll get to the bottom of it. There's a reason all this is happening, and it has nothing to do with us."

Mrs. Pierce appeared in the doorway, inviting them inside. She was an older woman in her early sixties,

Luke guessed, hair done in a bun and very properly dressed. Her room was immaculate, lots of activities posted on the wall, but a little sparser than any of the rooms Julie had when she was teaching. There was still a lot of curriculum displayed in a very organized fashion. There were checkoff sheets and charts where students could earn badges and buttons and stars for meeting certain milestones. What it told Luke was that there was going to be a lot of student participation.

"Have a seat."

"Thanks for seeing us, Mrs. Pierce. I am Kiley's aunt, and Luke is her uncle. My brother married his sister, and Kiley is the youngest of their three that we have taken into our home."

"Yes, I was made aware of this. So sorry for your family's loss. How is Kiley adjusting?"

"She seems to be doing fine. She's very close to our youngest, Jessica."

"Oh yes, Jessica, what a little dear she is. I get to see her third and fourth periods since we trade off with the other second-grade class. So what can I tell you and what can you tell me about her academic performance?"

"Well, I haven't tested her, because that really wasn't something I thought I should do. I didn't want to influence your decisions. But I think she's very bright. She reads quite a bit, even at seven. She has a tablet that she uses, but we're careful about what media she gets exposed to."

"I wish more parents were like you. That's a good thing."

"And she seems to have an interest in butterflies and gardens. Her mother was quite a gardener. Used to maintain a beautiful rose and wildflower garden for her butterflies. I think Kiley probably is missing that."

"Well, what I'm going to do is not assign her any homework for the first few days. Then I'll give her a series of workbooks to go through. Once she turns those in, I'll be able to find out where she is on the curriculum scale. And if she needs some remedial things, I will let you know."

"Thank you. That sounds perfect. I was hoping something like that would be arranged."

"I also have a book on butterflies. If you wouldn't mind giving her this to read? Tell her it's from her new teacher? She might like that." Mrs. Pierce searched a bookshelf at her back and pulled out a large book with huge butterfly drawings, handing it to Julie.

"This is lovely. Thanks so much!"

Mrs. Pearce searched both of their faces. "I do have to mention one thing, and you're probably going to hear this multiple times, so you may not like this, but it's the reality of the situation. Since we're a private school, as you know since you are principal of our sister campus, we are careful about who gets admitted. You probably know that as well."

"Well, yes, but I don't make the determination. As far as I know, we've never turned anyone away at my school—"

"Perhaps you've not seen that selection process first-hand, Mrs. Paulsen. And I doubt you've ever experienced the kind of issue going on now involving your family."

Luke grabbed the arms of his chair and waited for bad news.

"It looks like there's some news breaking about your sister and brother?"

"Yes, we watched the newscast last night on Channel 4. Very disturbing. And I have to say completely hit us from left field. We have no idea where all this is coming from, but I promise you, it's a huge distortion and a manufactured story. I'm not sure whether it's coming from any reputable source either. So I just ask for your forbearance and patience in letting things play out how they're going to. I assure you, we aren't going to let this interfere with any of the kids' education."

"Well, just understand that we'll support you as much as we can. We're doing this for the children, after all. If it gets to be a problem, then we may have to look at other alternatives. We don't want parents pulling their children out due to unnecessary publicity."

"Other alternatives?" Luke asked.

Mrs. Pierce directed her answer to Luke. "We may request that she transfer to another school."

"Oh, really?" said Luke.

"This, of course, would also affect Jessica."

Luke's stomach started churning, and he felt like hitting something. This whole situation was blooming out of control quickly. He didn't like where it was going at all.

"Mrs. Pierce, Julie and I have discussed it, and it's very possible that there's some kind of intentional leakage of these crazy stories to somehow damage us. I assure you there is no validity to any of it. And we are very devoted and dedicated parents, working very hard to give these three orphan girls, our nieces, a warm loving family. It would be extremely disruptive for our kids to have to change schools and to have all five of them have to relocate and get used to something new instead of just the three. So I beg of you not to rush to conclusions until we know further what's behind all this. Trust me, there is someone or something pulling the strings behind this."

Mrs. Pierce appeared to be moved by Luke's argument. "I understand your concern, and we are going to do everything we can to help you bring all this to a conclusion. Thank you for stopping by, and we look forward to seeing Kiley in the class on Monday."

She stood, extending her hand. The meeting had taken less than five minutes, which was much shorter than any of the other meetings they had had with their girls' teachers. He felt she was being very careful and neutral in her stance, even though she professed to support them. He was worried and distressed as he walked out of the room but thanked her for her time.

Julie held the butterfly book under her arm as they walked down the hallway toward the second room, where Maron and Lindsey would be in the same classroom as Amy. They knew Amy's teacher, Connie Matum, and had enjoyed her tremendously since the school year had started.

But when Luke turned to Julie while they waited outside the door, he could see she was in tears.

"This is the hard part, Jules. We worry about stuff we probably shouldn't even have to. The news media is just crap. They just throw out anything they can find. But trust me, we've done nothing wrong, and I don't think Colin and Stephanie did either. It's all going to be discovered. Just have patience please. And don't worry about it."

"You could see how affected Mrs. Pierce was. I just don't know what to tell them. Of course we say that it's not true, but we don't even know who it is we're fighting or where they're getting this information from. It's just so odd. I am heartbroken for how this is affecting the kids."

"Isn't this a change, having Maron and Lindsey in the same class?" Luke asked her. They had received instructions that the appointments would only be with two teachers not three when they arrived.

"Well, if you remember, Amy's class is a little bit small, so they probably felt since Lindsey was new that they'd put her in the fifth-grade class instead of sixth grade. And I think having her in the same class with her sister and Amy is a good thing. So for whatever reason they changed it, I think it's for the best. I just hope it's challenging enough for her. But after she gets her bearings, we can request a change if we feel she can handle it. They don't have a special honors class here for fifth grade, like my school."

Connie Matum greeted them warmly, giving them each a hug and then ushering them inside. She sat them at her desk and quickly assumed the seat on the other side. Donning her red glasses which contrasted with her frizzy bright blonde hair, she pulled up her laptop and clicked open a document that she was reading.

Connie had been trained in Mississippi and had a deep drawl. "I've made a list of a couple of things here. I don't know what the school situation was up in Sonoma County. They went to public school?" she asked them.

"Yes," Julie said. "I believe it was a very good district, one of the best. At least that's what my brother said. He also told me that Lindsey had been recommended for extra advanced placement classes. And a possible star lane they called it, a pathway for gifted children."

"I see," Connie said, letting her red glasses slip down her nose. "What about Maron?"

"I don't know about Maron. I just was told that about Lindsey. Maron seems to be a little more sensitive and kind of relishes being the odd man out. At least in our group, that's the way it's worked out so far."

Luke thought Julie did a great job of summarizing some of the dynamics he'd been experiencing over the past week.

"And, Luke, you are the primary caregiver at home? Is that right?"

"Yes ma'am. I'm in the military, as you know, and I've been given several months to stay home with the girls and make sure everybody gets situated properly. This is a big change for all of us. I was lucky to be able to get the time to do so."

"Well, bless your heart. I respect the military. My first husband was a Navy pilot, my dad was Army, and we moved all over the South. So we're grateful for your service, Mr. Paulsen."

"Thank you. I appreciate that."

"How's that coming?" she asked with a dimpled smile. Her eyes flashed in his direction. "I know if my husband was taking care of the kids, well, let's just say I wouldn't allow it. But I got to hand it to you, you know these days, we have to be flexible, don't we?"

"Yes, ma'am. It's a lesson in being flexible and humble."

"How is Amy taking to all of this?" she asked the two of them.

"She and Lindsey are very close. The cousins have always loved spending time with each other. Now that they're together twenty-four seven, we'll see how it works out, but we're lucky in that our families were very close before, so hopefully, this will continue. I haven't seen any negative effects so far on either of our two kids. And my brother's kids seem to accept the life changes they were given very maturely for their age. I'm very proud of them all," said Julie.

"I like hearing that, Julie. Well, we're going to do whatever we can to make things comfortable for them and to challenge them with their learning. As you know, our curriculum is quite advanced, and Maron may feel at first that it's far ahead of where she's been taught before, but we'll deal with that as it comes, and if they'll need extra tutoring, I will let you know. It sounds to me that Lindsey won't have a problem at all with it, and if I feel she needs to be promoted further, I'll also let you know. I don't think you'll have to hire a tutor in either case since they've got the best one at home."

"Thank you, Connie. I appreciate that."

"Do you have any other questions for me because that's pretty much all I've got?" asked Connie.

Luke considered whether or not he should bring up the newscast from last night and decided to not mention it in case it was something she didn't feel was important. Unfortunately, Julie didn't agree and brought it up herself.

"I'm sure you've heard a little bit about the investigation into my brother and sister-in-law's deaths and certain implications that we were quite shocked to hear on the TV last night on the news. If you see anything occur in the classroom, our kids getting overly sensitive, or you sense any kind of teasing or bullying going on, which I would doubt would happen, but if there is anything like that that does occur, please let us know. Don't be afraid to contact us."

"Duly noted, Julie."

"I'm not sure how much we're going to tell the kids about the investigation, and not everybody is going to react the same way, so there's a possibility they could be told things that are completely inaccurate or distorted. I just want you to know, Connie, that Luke and I are working very hard to try to help the police get to the bottom of whatever it is they're looking at, and we're completely cooperating with them. We want to learn the reasons for our siblings' deaths just like they do. But if you were to listen to the newscasters, you might get another story. So if at any time you have a question about anything, please feel free to ask either one of us."

"Thank you, Julie. I didn't want to bring it up, but of course, it is the white elephant in the room, isn't it?"

"It is."

"I understand, and it must be extremely stressful not knowing all the facts and details. I'm sure it will all come to light. And I wish you the best of luck, especially for the girls' welfare. Consider me an ally."

Luke was delighted with this interview. When they left the room, he admitted, "Even if she should be passed up the chain, I like Connie, and I'd think hard before moving Lindsey. I think she's right where she belongs," he said.

"I tend to agree. It wasn't my decision, but someone was looking out for us with this change."

They were approximately forty-five minutes early for their appointment with Sampson Biggs, who hadn't arrived at the school yet. After checking with the front office staff, Luke and Julie decided to go grab a cup of coffee before meeting him.

They each had a small espresso and sat in the color-ful coffee house, listening to the screams of the espresso machines in the background and the chatter of students and the clickety-clack of laptop keys. It was a great hangout for the college-age group with a junior college two blocks away.

Luke approached the subject of the interviews and asked Julie how they had gone.

"I'm not sure really. They're not saying a lot. They're trying to be nice, but they're not saying a lot. And that has me concerned a bit. I like Mrs. Pierce. I think she'll be a very strict but a good teacher for Kiley, but I'm glad Jessica has Donna Spencer. I'd almost rather the two be in the same class, they are so close."

"I was wondering the same thing. It's going to be more intimidating having her in a class all by herself. We could suggest a change, if that's politically smart. Do you think it's worth pursuing?"

"I think both teachers are excellent as far as their qualifications, and I think they will both be very sensitive to helping blend the kids in. I'll need to think about it. We can ask for a change if we need to. Let's talk further on it before we decide, okay?"

"What are you not telling me?"

"Luke, I've never been in this kind of situation be-fore where I feel like I have to apologize for who we are or who our family is. I've never been on the defense like this, and it's a really icky feeling for me. Everything I did surrounding the schools and my teaching and my relationship with my parents was always smooth and respectful. Now I feel like there's this cloud over everything. It's just not something I'm used to. I hope the appointment, the meeting with Biggs turns out to be a little better than I'm afraid it's going to be."

Luke grabbed her hand and kissed it. "It is what it is, Julie, and whatever happens, like you told me when this whole thing began, we are family, and we will weather the storm together as a family."

"Thank you for that, Luke. It means a lot."

They returned to the school, and within minutes, Sampson Biggs asked Julie to come into the assistant principal's office. Luke stood as well.

"Would you mind if I sit in on the meeting, sir?"

Biggs stiffened and then returned a disapproving stare. "I'm not so sure that's a good idea, Luke. This is a private matter between me and Julie. If you insist, I'm going to have to allow it, but I strongly advise against it."

Julie turned to him. "It's okay. You wait here, and I'll be out in just a few minutes. I'll be fine."

"I know you'll be fine, Julie, and that's not what I'm worried about. But I want to be there anyway." Then Luke added, "As you know, we're going through quite a bit, and everything we're doing is a joint decision. I think it's a good idea that I sit in on the appointment, so I can help Julie deal with the decisions that she's making. *We're* making together."

"If you insist, I really can't refuse. Come on in." Mr. Biggs stood to the side after he opened the door to the office.

"I suppose you watched the news last night, didn't you?" Biggs started.

Julie and Luke took seats on the couch at the side when Biggs motioned in that direction. He took a chair at a forty-five-degree angle to them.

"Yes, we watched it. I'm in shock, Sampson, to be honest with you," Julie said.

"You haven't heard any of this before?" he asked.

"No. All of this is new."

Luke added, "We knew they were investigating this as a murder, but not that it was a murder-for-hire or that a family member was involved."

"I suppose police departments have their own ways of scoping out all theories. They have to investigate all possibilities, don't they? Maybe they were preserving their evidence, sources. We don't know."

"They certainly didn't do that," barked Luke. "Someone leaked a bogus report to the media, and we think it was done on purpose."

Julie's attempt to soften Luke's rant didn't appear to sway Biggs. "We're cooperating with the authorities.

Anything we can do to assist them, we're going to do it all. We have nothing to hide, Sampson."

His icy demeanor was disturbing. "Well, the district office has received inquiries about your job here, your position as principal, the length of time you've been here, and whether or not there had been any complaints filed against you. I looked up your records, of course, and this would be routine anyway for considering you for the superintendent job, and I discovered that you had some difficulty with a parent several years ago, a decade ago I think. This parent actually caused harm to your union representative, isn't that right?"

"He kidnapped both of us. The man was insane, just insane," Julie said.

"And he fixated on you in particular, Julie, isn't that correct?"

"Yes, and it all started because I noticed some behavior in their child, Corey, that was unusual. It was also very sexual in nature, and it's the sort of thing that a teacher's supposed to report. You know, by law, I must report this in California. However, Mr. Miller objected to it. He attempted to sue the school district, as well as myself personally, until it was discovered that actually he was the perpetrator and was, in fact, a pedophile. I believe he's serving time today."

"It's a wonder you even want to teach with an experience like that. What can you tell me about that?" he asked.

"I did my job, Mr. Biggs. I didn't back down, even in the face of this horrible situation. I protected a young child from his father's preying actions. I don't need to justify my behavior."

"Yes, and I agree and commend you."

Luke noted his eyes were still cold. He was not convinced the man was telling the truth.

"I'm asking how you handle the stress of this?"

Julie thought for a moment and then answered. "Well, I compartmentalize it as being a fluke occurrence that, hopefully, will never occur again. I was right, Sampson. I did the right thing even in the face of unspeakable acts and behaviors of others. I like to think I was the calming person throughout all this."

"But you lost your colleague—"

Luke was livid. "What are you implying?"

"Have you ever had second thoughts? Do you take any responsibility for his overreaction that caused the death of another educator? Your union rep?"

"You mean, do I take responsibility for trying to shelter a young child who was being preyed on by a despicable human being? Absolutely not. My conscience is clear. If there were another way, I would have taken it. But how can I be responsible for a deranged parent? I stopped him. His daughter has a chance to be safe now, to rebuild her life. I hope she is getting the care she needs. She was the loser in all this, and I kept her safe."

Biggs paused. "And yet look at what has happened with your brother and sister. Have the police interviewed you at all about their claim of financial gain? Have you personally, you and Luke, profited from their deaths?"

Julie stood. Luke thought perhaps she'd clock him. He tugged on her hand but did not rise to threaten the man.

"Mr. Biggs, I'm sorry, but due to the nature of the investigation, we've been asked not to discuss it with other people. And all I could say is the sweeping generalizations the newscaster came up with last night are so bizarre, so completely inaccurate, we don't even know how to respond to it. But rest assured, we are going to get to the bottom of it, and we will find the person responsible for creating this situation. In the meantime, we want to let the police and the authorities do their job, so coming up with ideas or justifications for whatever may or may not have occurred isn't helpful. But just understand that we've done nothing wrong, and we don't believe my sister and her brother did either. But we will find out who is causing this."

Biggs leaned back into his high-backed swivel chair, lacing his fingers in front of him, glancing back and forth between both of them. "Well, I'm satisfied for now. Let's just see how things play out. I'm sure I don't have to tell you, Julie, that if there's any kind of controversy that follows you into the possibility of obtaining the superintendent's job, it's going to be a detriment to you getting that job. So let's hope it can all be handled quietly and quickly. And I'm so sorry all this is happening to you both. I truly am."

Luke wasn't sure he was telling the truth, but at least everybody knew where they stood. He hoped he didn't have to gear up for an emotional fight. But if it came to that, he knew he could step up to the plate. The most important thing in his life was his family, and nothing was going to touch or damage them.

Even if it cost him his Trident.

CHAPTER 12

J ULIE TRIED TO conduct her daily affairs as best she could but found herself fielding more phone calls than usual. Although people didn't come out and ask her what was going on, the increased frequency of their calls set Julie's radar on edge, and she knew the reason for their communications was partly to gain some information about the investigation without asking her directly.

She read over the trust documents she had taken in her briefcase, thinking it might make her feel better to do *something*. She found several things that concerned her and decided to call the bank to ask them about closing the account for Stephanie's business.

"I'm inquiring about my sister-in-law's closed business account, and I was wondering if you could help me with the details."

After giving the clerk some information, informing her she was the executor of the estate, she was directed to the branch manager.

"Who is this calling please?" the manager asked.

"My name is Julie Paulsen. My sister-in-law, Stephanie Christensen, managed this business account, and I'm in charge of the trust. I'm trying to figure out exactly where the money went when the account was closed. All I have is the checking account statement that showed a balance of about $34,000 in it. But I don't know where that money went when it was closed, and it happened to be closed on the day of her death."

"I see. Well, I'm afraid I'm limited in what I can give you, but if you are the executor of the estate, you can come in here with your paperwork, and I can see if I can release that information to you."

"Well, I live in San Diego, and your branch is in Santa Rosa. Do you have anything in the Southern California area?"

"We have several branches in Los Angeles, but none in San Diego. I'm fairly sure that in order to show the disposition of the funds, you would need to come to this branch where she opened the account. I'm not sure another branch would be able to give you that information, but I can check on it for you if you like. Give me your phone number and email address, and I will get back to you."

Julie didn't want to upset an already buzzing bee-hive so declined giving him any information. She knew it was probably something he might think about and question later on, but she wasn't interested in violating any of the rules that Clark Riverton and Gus Mayfield had laid down for them. She wanted to make sure they didn't get further embroiled. But if she could do some checking without making things worse, she figured that was not a bad idea.

Instead, this one appeared to be a dead end.

"I'm sorry, but let me talk to my attorney, and perhaps his office can initiate something for me. I apologize for taking your time. Good day."

Both she and Luke were interested in what Mayfield and Riverton had found out. She wondered if they actually did travel up to Northern California. She put in a call to the attorney who handled the trust in Santa Rosa.

"How are things going, Julie?" he asked her.

"Well, I don't know if you've heard the news, but the police are investigating Steph and Colin's accident as a murder. And they're looking for some kind of connection. If you can believe the newscasts down here anyway, it sounds like they're looking for somebody who thought they would financially gain from their death. The long implication of this is that I'm under some kind of suspicion."

"Oh dear. I am so sorry about that. I've been questioned as well, but they didn't give me this context."

"Who is 'they' anyway?" Julie asked.

"Well, he was an investigator with the State of California, I believe. I think I've got his card."

"He came to your office?"

"It's something that happens quite frequently when you handle trusts and estates. There are lots of other parties sometimes who don't want to surface right away. It could be someone, a distant relative just trying to do some poking around to see if they can find something they can make a case out of. I often don't divulge much information, and certainly in this case, I was very discreet. Let me see if I can find his card."

Julie waited.

"Okay, here it is. His name is Justin Hamblin, and I have his phone number if you'd like it."

"Please."

The attorney rattled off a phone number, beginning with an area code in the San Jose Peninsula area.

"Thank you."

"Do you recognize this fellow?"

"No, I don't. And I don't believe Colin or Stephanie has ever mentioned his name either."

"Anything else I can do for you?"

"Well, I was going through some of the bank accounts and documents, and I see that Steph's business account, which is what's causing all this issue in the news, had over $30,000 in it at the time of its closing.

And I can see from the statements that the closure happened, oddly enough, on the day they were killed. I'm wondering if you can tell me where this money wound up, because I don't see it deposited in any of their other bank accounts."

"Maybe they cashed it. People do that."

"I thought of that, but the bank won't give me any details. And they're saying I have to show up in person in order to get that information, even though I'm the executor of their estate."

"Well, maybe he thinks that since it was something that happened before—"

"But do we know that, really? And if the police are looking into this as being a murder-for-hire, should I give this information to the police or should I just launch our own investigation?"

"I see. Well, I always tell my clients to fully cooperate."

"And I am. I just discovered this large sum of money today when I was reviewing the accounts. And I didn't notice before that it was closed the day of their accident, not before. So it really isn't a stretch. If they wanted to be fully transparent, they'd release that information at least to you, wouldn't they, as their attorney?"

"I hesitate to get involved, especially if I could be accused later on of trying to impede the police's investigation, so I'd advise you to contact the police. The problem is, who do you talk to? And you need to be careful about this. Not everything that's given to them is followed up on. They are understaffed and overwhelmed with cases. So you're going to want to be careful. But it's a valid question, and something you should know. And if there's thirty-some-thousand dollars cash missing, as executor of the estate, on behalf of the children, you owe them a duty to discover it. That's my opinion anyway. So I think you should try to do that and then turn over what you found to the police. But make sure you are talking to the head investigation team, not someone else."

"'Someone else' being this Hamblin fellow?" Julie asked him.

"Yes, I've seen cards like this before, and I can't tell you that I really think it's legitimate. He may not be working for the State of California. He may be working for someone else. And I didn't spend any time checking on him, but if you like, I can have our own investigator look into his background, and I can get back to you."

"If you would, please. Thank you so much. And I think I'm going to take your advice. My husband has some close friends down here in San Diego, one who used to be with the crime task force and another gentleman who's a retired sheriff. They have lots of contacts even in Northern California. I think I'm going to have them make some inquiries for us as well."

"Well, I'll let you know what we find out, and you take care."

Julie had to ask him one more question. "Did you ever get the sense that Stephanie and Colin were involved in something shady or nefarious?"

"What makes you say that?"

"We found a bunch of things for her home-based business that were... Well, she was selling sex toys, okay?"

"Oh dear. Really? That doesn't sound like Steph at all."

"I think it was just sort of a fun thing she did to earn some extra money, but she never told me about it. And it looks like she made quite a bit of money with it, especially recently. I'm wondering if all this is related. Did you ever get any inkling they were involved in something that could be illegal?"

"As in child pornography like the news media says?"

"Exactly. I agree with you, that's so out of character for them. Did you see anything that caused you to be suspicious?"

"Julie, I couldn't have been more proud of Stephanie if she was my own daughter. I never got even a wrinkle of an idea about her being involved in something. And Colin, well, he's just one of those good guys, a really great guy, and I doubt he would ever put his family in some kind of trouble. So I doubt he would ever be involved in something like this. Someone is pulling the strings here, and I don't think you need to take more than two seconds to even concern yourself about whether or not your sister-in-law and brother were involved. It's just impossible."

Armed with that information, Julie felt slightly buoyed. It didn't take all of the weight off, but he was a professional. He had worked with Colin and Stephanie before, and he could attest to their character in his long-standing position with them. He was going to be one of the good guys with the white hats on their side. She was lucky that they had such an ally.

She decided to come home early, cutting it off about two o'clock in the afternoon. She texted Luke before she left the school.

"Coming home early. I think I have a little bit of good news."

His return text upset her.

"That's good. Because my news isn't so good. Come home safely, and watch your surroundings. Eyes in the back of your head, Julie. We'll talk more when you get here."

CHAPTER 13

W HAT WAS IT, Luke thought, that made women so much more flexible and resilient to deal with family stress, horrible things, taking care of children, and maintaining the household? He wondered what gene they had that allowed them to carry on, because he was going completely batshit crazy holding all this negativity, all this darkness, this huge gray cloud of crap in his gut while trying to smile and laugh and participate with five little innocent girls he would die for.

If he didn't get it together, they'd pick up on all his worry and darkness. Julie always made everything look so easy, so simple. If she was upset about something, the girls were the last to know—unless she wanted them to know, and then she'd lower the boom, but somehow with a sprinkle of sugar and fairy dust. Luke couldn't do that.

He'd known guys who had cheated on their wives

before, had gambling problems, or did drugs and kept it from their wives. They had a policy on the teams not to tattle on another man, unless someone's health and safety were at stake. If the law was being broken, if someone was headed for a fall, a suicide, or to commit a crime, it usually wasn't a hard decision to make, given all the circumstances.

He knew, in the end, all things were made clear, and a lot of wives had to put up with that crap and carry on as if their whole world hadn't just gotten blown up. He couldn't do that. He really couldn't do that. "Moving on" wasn't something he did, and he'd tried too.

Like the guilt he felt for the accident that took Camilla's life. He'd never get over that totally. It would be with him for the rest of his life. He'd learned to live with it. But moving on? No such thing in Luke's world. And if you did dumb shit, well, you'd pay the price forever.

Forever.

What they tried to train for was being able to endure forever, exercise and mentally plan for it, because it was the nature of his job.

He was trained to fight, yes, and be a warrior, but he wasn't trained to deal with the hot, oily boiling pit in his stomach while he was looking at five little girls sitting out on the lawn under an umbrella dancing to music, wearing sunglasses and laughing, lying on their bellies, and kicking their legs up while jumping in their little wading pool, just being normal little girls. And Luke was sitting here watching them with tears streaming down his cheeks, tears he never wanted to ever show them.

He was crushed, nearly to the point of feeling defeat. The problem was, he didn't know who to fight and how to find out about it. The waiting was killing him, and the maintaining a cool and happy "happy-happy" demeanor was just driving him crazy.

Even Riverton calling to give him an update didn't help. He didn't want to tell him about his concerns, about what he had seen on Stephanie's clipboard. He didn't want to call up Dr. Brownlee and tell him either. He didn't want to tell Julie. Why couldn't he just wipe all this out of his mind and play with the girls? Just be with the girls, clean the sink, do the dishes, do the laundry? He should pretend that everything was hunky-dory-Disneyland-sparkly-great. Why couldn't he pretend?

And that was the issue for him. He wasn't made for this. He was made for something else. And did that disqualify him from being a normal human being, a father, a husband? He wanted to blast whoever it was that had ruined their family life, however temporary it might be. Every hour and every minute, it got worse.

Before Riverton's call, he'd dared to look through the box he'd brought home from the storage, like he was drawn to it as a moth was to the flame. Why the fuck did he think this was a good idea? He picked up the clipboard he had taken, and underneath all the orders and paperwork that he had quickly glanced through earlier was a list of Steph's customers. It was a long list, and it also had numbers, amounts of purchases. His finger traveled down the list of unknown customers, mostly women's names, until he came to one particular purchaser who had made enormous purchases, like thousands and thousands of dollars' worth of purchases.

His hands shook as he read the entry. It was the Feathers and Tails Ranch, a well-known bordello in Las Vegas.

When he came upon it, his heart had sank down to his ankles. His mouth had been parched and he ached, just ached all over. He knew about this place, although he'd never been there. It was a raunchy, horrible, dirty place with despicable acts and girls who were clearly damaged. He'd heard tales about it, and nobody he cared for or spent any time with had ever been there, but they'd all heard about it.

Now he was ashamed to say he'd never done anything to try to interfere with their business, because they had talked about it before, he and his friends, about how it just seemed like the wrong kind of place and should be looked into. The girls were reported to be all foreign and very, very young. Perhaps illegal. But something had been protecting the business. Some cretin, some monster, or a group of monsters were making money.

But they also were buying from his sister. And that bothered him most of all.

Was this group Stephanie's secret partner? Were they the real people behind her business? Were Stephanie and Colin being used for their squeaky cleanness? His mind was racing with all the possibilities. He just didn't want to utter them to anybody for fear of actually making them come true. Like, if he mentioned it or he spoke about it, all of a sudden it became real. Whereas, right now, it was just some crazy ass idea running around bouncing off the sides of his skull.

He looked out at the little girls again and felt the hot tears drip onto his shirt. The person he needed to be and the person he was this afternoon were two completely different beings. He wished he hadn't seen so much of the ugliness that he had seen during wartime, the women and children caught in the crossfire, the little boys forced to stand up and hold guns that were big enough to make them fall over. He'd seen tanks overrun schools and villages, kids with their arms cut off after the SEALs had done a vaccination clinic.

But even those things he could compartmentalize and put aside for now. Because that was his training. Because he went out on the battlefield, and the lines were drawn clearly. He knew what side he was on. This, all this stuff, this degrading bullshit that was going on and invading his happy family life, this was some kind of a ghost, an angry gray cloud that just wouldn't leave him alone.

It was almost like all the innocent people he couldn't save were pulling at his feet from the grave. He saw Camilla as he held her—his pregnant first wife, dying in his arms. He saw the boys overseas he couldn't save. He saw his SEAL buddies and interpreters who had been returned to their camp mutilated, bloodied, and tortured. It kept him awake at night, but he knew it was his ticket to play, the cost of his heroism forever. He just didn't like being that close to death.

But with this, this was just evil. He was on the prec-ipice. It was like staring over the edge of a 15-story building and taking forever to decide to jump, causing pain, the worry of what will happen to all these little girls, what was happening to all the other people who were being victimized and subjugated.

It was proof he couldn't save everybody, and that was the biggest problem. He didn't know who to get help from, and to solve it, who to attack, who to kill.

"Luke, you've got to get a handle on yourself." Hearing his own voice didn't help, though.

When Riverton's call came in, he threw the clipboard on the bed and answered. "Tell me something good. I need something good right now, Clark."

"Oh my God, Luke, are you all right?"

"The simple answer? No. Please tell me you found something that we can go on something where we can help end all this. It's a nightmare, Clark."

"Hey, Luke, calm down. You need to settle yourself. You aren't going to be able to get through all this unless you can settle yourself. So let me tell you what I got, and then you call somebody who can be more warm and fuzzy with you, Luke, because I don't know if this is good news or bad news."

"Just spill, Clark."

"I reached out to some old contacts in Sonoma County, who are agreeing to cooperate with me a little bit. I can't get shit out of the highway patrol, but my source in Santa Rosa is considering bringing in the FBI. And I don't know if that'll make it better or worse, but at least we'll get some deeper roots and see if we can't find out where this is leading."

"Okay, so exactly what are you saying? Can you spell it out for me please? I'm having a hard time being logical."

He saw Maron doing a little ballet step, a performance for the other girls, and the four of them clapped for her while she took a bow. Such a beautiful sight on any other day except today. Those five little innocent girls deserved everything in the world, and Luke wanted to give them everything he could.

"So tell me now, dammit."

"Well, it appears that there were some problems with Steph's business. There were some accounts and orders that got placed under her name that she disputed with the company. Apparently, they were at a convention in Las Vegas when they discovered all this. Something they uncovered got them so upset that they canceled a scheduled speech. Steph was going to be participating on a panel for this company she worked for, and she decided not to show up. They left early. And it looks like they made one stop before they left. By checking her phone records, it looks like she went to a bank, and then they got in their car for the drive home. That's all I've got."

"Okay. What do they think it means?"

"Well, she closed the account, apparently, making a large withdrawal. And we have not been able to verify from the bank in Las Vegas why. They haven't been contacted yet. We're waiting on the FBI to do that. But they're about to."

"So her bank in Santa Rosa had a branch in Las Vegas?"

"No, not exactly. I'm not sure why they used that bank."

"So what is this BS about someone taking financial advantage of her, insinuating that it's Julie and me?"

"That hasn't come from the police. We don't think the police investigation is compromised. So I don't want you to worry about that."

"But, Clark, they're calling Kyle. We just found out yesterday they've contacted the school board. People are asking questions. There's all kinds of information getting out to the news media. Where is this coming from?"

"I can't tell you that. But I can tell you this, Luke, you need to get yourself a criminal attorney and right away. I can recommend somebody if you like, but you need to get a high-powered very visible attorney who is good with social media."

After Riverton's call, he straightened the bedroom and placed the clipboard back in the box, folded clothes, and put in another load of laundry. He took out food for dinner, hamburger meat and noodles for a stroganoff, and picked some tomatoes and lettuce in the garden for a salad, waving to the girls as he did so.

That was his shell moving. Inside, he was completely crushed. When he got Julie's text, he was grateful she'd be home early. But he was dreading having to tell her about what Riverton disclosed. This was not going to be a normal family dinner. Nothing about his life was going to be normal ever again.

He decided to call Dr. Brownlee, who was not available. He left his phone number and knew he'd get a call back sometime today.

When he heard Julie's car pull up to the house, he closed his eyes and put his hand over his heart. He wasn't going to persevere for himself. He was going to do it for her. She deserved all of the success and accolades she had earned for so many years working through the system. She deserved to be able to come home and have someone greet her at the door and hold the rest of their life together. He wasn't worried about Julie. He was worried about himself.

Am I really up to all of this? What if I fail?

CHAPTER 14

JULIE HANDED LUKE the piece of paper with Justin Hamblin's name and phone number on it.

"This is the investigator who's been sniffing around the edges. I talked to the trust attorney, and he confirmed he spoke with this gentleman and that he doesn't think he's legitimately involved in the investigation. I think this is where our leaks are coming from."

"Who is he?" asked Luke.

"We don't know. But I think it would be good to give to Mayfield and Riverton, although the trust attorney is putting his private investigator on it as well. He said he worked for the State of California, but his card doesn't say what division. It may take a while, but if he's legitimate, we'll be able to find him. If he's not, then this is a huge clue for us. I feel hopeful we're finally getting to the bottom of what's going on."

"That's good, Jules. That's really good news."

She saw that Luke was un-showered and hadn't shaved today. She checked the outside window and saw the girls sitting down at the table doing some workbooks and reading. Everything looked under control with the house. She smelled dinner cooking in the kitchen. It was just Luke and his appearance that bothered her the most.

She walked up to him and placed her palms on either side of his cheeks. "What is it, Luke? What's going on?"

"I talked to Clark today, and they've determined there was some kind of a convention change for Steph and Colin. They were supposed to speak somewhere, and instead, they left the convention early. They stopped at a bank on their way home. Except they never made it here, did they?"

"What bank?"

"Well, he didn't tell me what bank, just got it from the locator on her phone. That's what they're trying to find out. Riverton said the police in Santa Rosa are going to call in the FBI, and it's probably not one of the banks that Steph and Colin bank with. It's some other bank. But that was the last stop they made before they came home."

"Okay, well, that's good news then. I think we're getting closer to something, Luke."

"I don't know. There's something else, though."

"What?"

"I went through the clipboard and looked at her customer list, and I found an entry to a particular purchaser who happened to buy thousands of dollars' worth of goods this last month. It's all recent purchases."

"Okay. What are you saying?"

"It's not an individual. It's a ranch, a bordello in Las Vegas. It's a very famous one, in that it's on the lower end. There's been a lot of rumors and talk about it for years, but it's still in operation. And this particular bordello is known for having very young-looking prostitutes that work there supposedly legally. But most of them are foreign, and the thought is that perhaps many of them have been trafficked from other countries and are not really legal here in the United States. They are being used. It looks on the surface, Julie, that they could be Colin and Steph's secret partners. And somebody needs to know about it."

"Well, I think you should tell everybody. I mean, what did Riverton say?"

"Julie, he said there were orders placed under Steph's name that she disputed with the company. And when she stopped and closed her account out, she did so from a different bank. We don't know where the money went to. That's why they are bringing in the FBI."

"Well, that's good news. That jives with what I discovered. I was looking through the records, and I saw she'd made a $34,000 withdrawal. I also didn't know where that money went, so I asked our attorney, and that's when he told me about the investigator that came to see him. We've got this guy's name and number. Now let's go get him looked at. Let's check him out. Can Clark or Gus do that?" she asked.

"Yes, and there's one more thing. Clark recommended that we get a criminal attorney. Somebody very high-powered. That's going to cost a lot of money, Julie."

"How much?" Julie asked.

"I talked to the office Riverton recommended. His assistant is insisting on a retainer of $25,000. That's going to wipe out our savings."

"Well, I'm hoping we won't need all of it. But if Riverton thinks it's necessary, I think we better do it. I hate to pay that much money for attorney's fees, but somebody's doing a pretty good job of smearing us, and I think it's the only way we can fight back. We can't do it ourselves, Luke. It'd be like sending me out on the battlefield with your equipment. I wouldn't know the first thing on how to use it. We need to hire somebody who knows what they're doing. We need to hire somebody who's competent and runs across this every day. Let's go see him tomorrow."

"Well, tomorrow's Saturday, so I don't think we'll be able to get in until Monday. But maybe after we drop the kids off, we could do that."

"Luke, I just want to say to you, however it works out, if everything goes away, we still tried to do the right thing. That's the most important thing to remember. We're not fighting for us. We're fighting for the girls." She took his hand and walked him to the dining room picture window so he could look at all five of them sitting on the patio.

"These are the kids you fought for when you went overseas. These are the kids we're fighting for now. I don't care who is behind this or how big and powerful they are. Whatever it costs us, I will willingly do it to keep them safe."

Luke grabbed her in his arms, and for the first time in their married life, he sobbed into her chest.

"I'm sorry, Julie. So grateful for you. I can't help it."

"This doesn't mean you're weak, Sweetheart. It means you're a human being. And I, for one, love you for it. We will get through this. I promise, Luke, we will."

THE FIRST DAY back at school for the girls was exciting for everybody. Luke and Julie took them all on a shopping spree over the weekend, buying new clothes, backpacks, notebooks, shoes, and socks, everything to make them feel like it was Christmas all over again. They had planned on perhaps overspending, but it wasn't just for the girls they did it. It was for them as well. Things had been so tight, they'd been so careful with the budgeting, they just decided to splurge, maybe one last time, on the girls. It was an all or nothing thing for Julie. Luke completely agreed.

There were no fights over the weekend over who was going to sleep where. They didn't care where their clothes were hung, which closet, or which drawer they got. The girls were just happy to have so many beautiful new things. And even if they'd had a Christmas tree in their downstairs living room, it wouldn't have felt more festive. It really was something Julie needed to see.

They walked Amy, Maron, and Lindsey into their classroom and introduced them to their teacher, Connie Matum. Amy did a good job walking them around the room, introducing them to some of her friends and some of their new schoolmates. Kiley and Jessica stayed behind, watching from the doorway, holding hands.

Then they took the younger two girls over to Kiley's room. Before going to the new classroom, she had Kiley return the butterfly book.

"Thank you very much, Mrs. Pierce. I really enjoyed the book. I read it three times over the weekend."

Mrs. Pierce was a little bit on the frosty side, but after it was explained why they were going together, she had fully embraced the idea that the two girls would be in the same class. Luke and Julie both gave a hug and kiss to Jessica and Kiley and walked down the hall toward their car holding hands.

"Well, my dear," started Luke, "this is going to be a very interesting day, isn't it?"

"It's always an interesting day with you, Luke. I don't care what anybody thinks about me or my family. All I care about is what we've done together and what our future looks like. Whatever this guy says, I'll somehow endure it, within reason."

"Well, look at it this way, Julie, if we had to, we could raise a little money selling off those twelve boxes, right?"

"Oh, Luke, you're so bad. I'm going to tell all your friends about that."

"They'd probably agree with me, Julie. But you go ahead if you think you're bold enough to do that."

"You bet I am. I need a little comic relief. I hope this guy is the right choice, but if he's not, I'm going to get the satisfaction of firing Mr. Cornelius Goodman. I never thought I would talk to that guy. I hate his billboards and commercials."

"It probably works for him."

"He's a trained killer."

"That's what we want, baby. He's attorney to the stars, to professional athletes, and celebrities. But he's a good friend of Riverton, so I think he ought to be a safe bet. Shall we go, my dear?" he asked, opening the door for her.

They drove up to Los Angeles and headed to a tall steel and glass office building off of Wilshire Boulevard. It had a sweeping view of the city, at least what they could see. Still, it was a dramatic skyscape. Cornelius Goodman's firm had over sixty attorneys on staff, every single one of them listed, taking up a whole floor of the building. They pressed floor 48 and were taken in an express elevator right to his offices.

The attractive young woman at the front desk could have been an actress herself or a high fashion model. She professionally greeted them by name, handed them a small questionnaire packet, and discreetly slipped them into a conference room overlooking the city. Then she drew the drapes so the rest of the office couldn't peer in. Julie figured that was probably the protocol she was trained to do in dealing with some of the high-profile clients he worked with.

"You know, with all those attorneys in his firm. I think we'll probably be dealing with somebody else. But we'll see."

"Whatever he recommends, I'm going to do it. Didn't you say that?"

"Yes, I did."

Roughly five minutes after they completed their forms, Mr. Cornelius himself entered the door. He was easily six foot six, impeccably dressed all the way down to his expensive silk tie and matching handkerchief. With his height and his extreme good looks, Julie knew that he was a formidable opponent in a courtroom.

The first thing out of his mouth was directing them to stay seated.

"I got you here. You're in my office. You've had all kinds of stress put on you, but this is going to be day one of your emancipation."

Julie thought it was a rather bold statement to make.

Luke chuckled. "Well, I kind of like that. That's almost worth $25,000 right there."

Mr. Goodman sat and slapped his portfolio book on the glass tabletop. "Mr. Paulsen, I understand you're one of the Navy's finest. And I want to let you know that I am also an elite warrior. I'll tell you two things about me. First of all, I was done a favor many years ago by a certain detective. I was headed on a path that wasn't going to get me what I got today." He turned around and displayed with his arms the beautiful view. "He told me that day that I better make good with the chance I've been given, and I had the opportunity to transform and help other people do the same.

I never forgot that, and anybody who Clark Riverton recommends to me gets my special treatment. In your case, Mr. Paulsen, since you have risked your life to protect my freedoms, I'm not going to charge you for this."

"What's the catch? Who do I have to off?" Luke said, jokingly. "Excuse me, that was not serious."

Julie gave him a disapproving stare. "Luke, that's—"

"It was funny, but I don't joke about murder, Mr. Paulsen. I know you don't either, really. But you're probably nervous, so I'll let it go. But yes, I am going to tell you that you're going to do some work for me. I want you to show up at every press conference. I want you not to be afraid of answering questions, as long as I'm there to coach you or you answer exactly as I prescribe. Is that clear?"

"Absolutely," Luke answered. Julie felt relieved.

"I'm going to tell you what to say and what not to say, and we're going to let the cops do their job and find whoever's messing with your family. Once we find them, Mr. Paulsen, Mrs. Paulsen, they aren't going to stand a chance. In my world, I know how to get it done. You guys need to just be good parents. You need to show up and do what I've told you. Now, I don't want any questions, I don't want any argument or your opinions about anything. I just want you to do 100% everything I tell you to do. Is that clear?"

Julie watched as his smile slowly widened. In fact, it was such a bright, wide smile it was disarming. She also noted he was studying them both very carefully and watching their reaction. She wondered what he was looking for.

Luke and Julie returned a glance at each other. Luke spoke up next, "Mr. Goodman, we will be your grunts. I promise you, you're not going to get any flak from us. We know how to take orders. And we know when we're outmatched. I'm going to rely on you to be the expert. Both of us are. Whatever it takes, sir. Whatever it takes. As long as I don't have to get my long guns out and ruin my career or hurt my family, it's whatever it takes."

CHAPTER 15

LUKE PICKED UP Mr. and Mrs. Christensen at the San Diego Airport.

"How was your flight?" he asked them.

They looked tired but happy to have landed.

"Oh, they just keep making those seats smaller and smaller, don't they?" Melanie Christensen said to him. "And I told him we should spring for First Class, but—"

Luke finished it for her. "It didn't feel like a celebration coming here, did it?"

Julie's dad covered quickly. "No, Luke, that has nothing to do with it. I'm just cheap, that's all. Trying to make sure our money lasts until we kick the can, you know. It's just, you know you're not going to live forever, but your bills do. They never expire, do they?"

"Well, Julie's delighted you're here. I already texted her, and she's waiting for you at home."

"She's at home today? Isn't this a school day?" Mrs. Christensen asked.

"Not today. She took the day off especially because you're coming."

On the way home, Luke stopped for a couple of things Julie asked him to get. "Do you need anything at the store? I'll be right back if not?"

"We're good."

Her parents both sat in the back seat of his Hummer. They looked smaller than he remembered, but they were as in love as they'd been in high school when they met. Luke had heard the stories.

"Good enough, then. I'll be right back."

On the way into the market, he got a call from Gus Mayfield.

"Well, I'll tell you what, Luke, that press conference was one hell of a show. How'd you get Cornelius Goodman?"

"Didn't Riverton tell you? He referred him to us."

"Did you have to mortgage your house to hire him?"

"Not telling. I got secrets too. But he cut us a good deal. So you have news for us?"

"I do, and I've talked to the trust attorney. We're going to be launching an investigation into bank fraud, and I've let him know the bank in Las Vegas is very likely going to be served and raided by the feds. Now don't tell anybody, but it's due to happen in the next day or two. I can't believe how fast all of this has gone.

I think the fact that you guys were so public and on TV so much really spurred a few wheels to start turning faster than they normally would have, if you get my drift."

"I get you. Goodman told us so. He said, 'the crickets come out of the field.' I don't think law enforcement likes a lot of publicity, do they?"

"Well, I like the way he did it, Luke. He didn't blame the locals who were looking into it. He just said the FBI had more resources than he did and it was going to be a much larger investigation. I think, when they hear that, they all go running back to their desks and make sure every I is dotted, every T is crossed. And what do you know, they found something. I don't know what they found, but apparently, they're pretty sure they found a bank in Las Vegas that has been participating in some strange activity. And that's all I'm going to say."

"Hey, thanks, Gus. We needed some good news."

"So how's everything else going?" he asked Luke.

"The girls are settling in really well at school. And they love their classes. I think Julie's the one struggling right now a bit. But hopefully, that'll be behind us soon."

"I heard she didn't get the superintendent's job. That's too bad."

"It's their loss. She would've been perfect for that

job, and she's already had offers from other parts of the country. Not that we want to move. But it's going to be okay. We agreed when all this started that, whatever the outcome, it was going to be okay."

"Well, I don't want to take too much of your time. I just thought I'd let you know stay tuned to the news, because there'll probably be some pretty soon. Either that or Cornelius will think up something. I don't think that man wants to go a day or two without getting his face in the headlines. But whatever it takes. All I can say is I could never afford him. Must be costing you a fortune."

"Doesn't matter, Gus. Whatever, it's worth it. My family's worth it."

"That's great to hear, Son. Well, you keep me posted, and I'll make sure to let you know if we run across anything else that you need to know. My best to Julie."

Driving up to the home, Julie ran from the front steps, hugging her mother and father. The girls followed behind her, everybody jumping up and down to get a hug with Grandma or Grandpa. Everyone talked to them, interrupting each other almost to the point of arguing who could tell their stories first. Luke could see that Julie's parents were invigorated with the group, and their travel malaise was completely wiped away by the energy coming from the girls. Like a bunch of elves guiding a giant, the girls took their grandmother and grandfather up the steps, through the front door, and into the living room. Two of them carried their suitcases upstairs while the others led them into the bedrooms that they occupied.

Luke heard the suitcases hitting the walls, but he didn't care. All that could be fixed with paint and a little time.

He listened while they showed them the bunk beds and the posters and the coloring and all the things they had done to decorate their rooms. Luke stood at the bottom of the stairway listening to the happy activity. It was everything he'd thought about being together would be. The only trouble was, it may not last. But he decided to enjoy it for the moment anyway.

He walked into the kitchen where Julie had retreated.

She was bending over the oven, pulling some dinner rolls out, her rear end poking out of that flowered apron that Luke used to wear.

He was enjoying the view. *To heck with the dinner rolls.*

"I almost burned these darn things. You'd think I'd never spent any time in the kitchen. I'm actually rusty, Luke." She closed the door, setting the well-cooked rolls on the stovetop. She pushed the hair from her forehead and greeted him with her arms wide, both her hands encrusted in flowered, quilted oven mitts that matched her apron.

"Where did you get those?" Luke asked.

"They were in the bottom drawer where the apron usually is."

"I never knew they were there. I would've used them too."

She walked up to Luke, pulled her arms around his torso, and brought him in against her. Whispering, she said, "I'm going to buy you a manly pair, very manly, and a manly apron for you to wear. I think you need that."

"Well, I'll accept your gift of manly oven mitts and an apron, if you'll accept my gift I've left for you upstairs."

"Really?" she asked.

"While you guys were shopping for school clothes, I went to a specialty shop. I won't tell you which, but you'll know when you see it."

"In a pink box?" she asked.

"Yeah, but it's not one of Steph's. Trust me on that."

She hugged him close and whispered, "I didn't think so, Sweetheart."

He helped her set the table, and he was amazed that everybody could fit with the extensions they hadn't used since they'd bought the table years ago.

Julie's parents arrived with their entourage encircling them, everybody vying for position to sit next to them.

Julie lit the candles and brought out the beautiful turkey she had been cooking all day. Luke helped her with all the other things, including the rolls, which were still well-done but very warmly received.

Mr. Christensen remarked, "Is it Thanksgiving? That's not for another month!"

"We are thankful, Luke and me and all the girls. We're thankful we could celebrate this nice dinner with you people today. We're so excited you came to visit, and we can't wait to show you all the wonderful things we love about San Diego, right, girls?"

A cheer erupted from all parts of the table.

Luke said grace, but before he began to carve the turkey, Julie stopped him.

"I just wanted to take a couple of moments and think about Stephanie and Colin. I wish they could be here today. I know they would've loved seeing you guys so happy, loved seeing you, Mom and Dad, and it's one of the reasons why we invited you up this weekend. I have a special family, and I never knew it until this all happened. I never doubted we were raised in love, and I never doubted how lovingly you were raised with Stephanie and Colin. I knew our girls loved each other, and I knew it was going to work. And we have a long ways ahead of us, but I'm very grateful, and that's why this is Thanksgiving for me, and hopefully, you can share in it too."

Luke came around the corner and gave her a big hug. Little Jessica squirmed out of her chair and did the same, which was so appropriate and consistent with the way she gave affection.

As he began cutting the turkey, Julie added one more note.

"Next year, we're going to need a highchair at this table."

Luke dropped the carving knife and paring fork and stared at his wife.

The girls looked confused, but Mr. and Mrs. Christensen were up on their feet, giving Julie a hug. Grandpa Christensen explained it to the girls. "You're going to have a little sister or a brother."

"Probably a sister," Luke said, smiling. "I don't think we make boys in this family. We make girls. We make beautiful girls. And I wouldn't have it any other way."

CHAPTER 16

JULIE FINGERED THE beautiful white, lacy nightgown Luke had purchased for her, laid out prettily on her side of the bed. He came up behind her, wrapped his arms around her, and kissed her neck.

"I wanted you to look beautiful tonight. You're not only a wonderful mother, you're a wonderful daughter, a wonderful teacher and principal—"

"Well, we have to talk about that."

"Okay, it's been a busy day, Julie, but go ahead. Tell me now."

"No, I loved where you were going with it, so complete your thought, and then we can talk later. Okay?"

"Okay. It sounds good. I wanted you to wear this, because I wanted you to know that, in addition to all those wonderful things, you are the most sexy woman in the whole world, and you should be wearing beautiful clothes, beautiful nighties. I just wanted you to have something special. I love you so much, and I owe you so much. This whole family owes you so much. I just wanted you to know you are cherished. You are loved beyond belief."

She was sobbing, but until he felt the hot tears cross over the backs of his hands wrapped around her, he didn't realize it. She hid it from him. She turned in his arms and looked up at him, placing her hands up around his neck.

"Luke, I'm so glad to see you're back. My Luke is back finally! We don't even have everything resolved, and you're back—the man I loved then and still love. We've weathered the worst part. I know there will be tough days ahead, but this makes me so happy."

"I've always been here, Jules. I really have."

"Yes, but you've not been able to express it. You jumped in, yes, but you've embraced our life, such as it is. I can't tell you how relieved I feel. It's been my honor and my complete pleasure. I'm overwhelmed with the love you have for this family. I'm over-whelmed with how you treat me. I feel like I'm the luckiest girl in the whole world. No matter what happens tomorrow, whatever happens in the future, I am always going to be your girl. And I couldn't have chosen a better partner for my life."

He planted a long, deep kiss on her lips. She was so hungry for him, smiling inside her heart at the knowledge that their love created another human being. And he didn't even flinch with the idea of having six children, maybe even six girls!

When they separated, he whispered in her ear, "How long have you known?"

"I think I got pregnant right away after we went up to Santa Rosa, and normally, I would've waited longer, but I knew Mom and Dad were coming, so I decided to get the blood test, and it confirmed it. Now it's still early, so a lot could happen, Luke. But I just wanted you to know. I wanted everyone to get some good news. No matter what else."

"So what is this going to do with the work situation?"

"Well, today, when I got the results, when the doctor's office called me, the next thing I received was this little letter in the mail." She went over to her nightstand and pulled out a letter from the school district.

Luke hesitated but then saw the letter had already been opened. She watched him read the words.

"You're going to let them get away with this?"

"No, a suspension means that I don't have to show up for work. It's a suspension with pay, Luke. We can take our time getting ready for the new baby, devoting ourselves full-time to whatever's happening next with the police investigation, and monitoring the inquiry into Steph and Colin's murder. I really think it's a blessing. I already knew I was pregnant. Then when I got this, I thought, this is perfect!"

Luke chuckled and then drew her into him again.

"How did I get so lucky? You talk about being so lucky. I'm the luckiest guy around. You're the only person in the world who would say a suspension was a good thing. You've been my rock, Julie. I never would have made it if it wasn't for you."

Julie knew she would remember their love making that night like it was the first time. And she remembered that one too. He was so tender with her, especially now that she was pregnant. Even though there wasn't anything he could do to disturb the baby, she knew men worried about that, and so his tenderness was extra special. And from her previous pregnancies, she also realized she would be horny as hell at least until she got to the six-month period. She'd already begun to feel her breasts getting fuller and had wonderful sensual dreams about motherhood, breastfeeding, the whole nine yards. She was so pleased her girls were so excited, all five of her girls, because she had really started thinking of Colin and Stephanie's girls as hers now.

She gave back all of the passion and tenderness he gave her, making sure he was fully satisfied by doing a few extra things that drew his attention or brought a smile to his face. She showed him how much she worshiped and honored him. His beautiful, muscled body enveloped her and made her soul sizzle. It had been so rare these past few months to feel the strength of him, and that always came with the damaged parts. But for now, she was grateful for this one night of strength, and love.

In the morning, Luke was off at a team meeting, since the group was going to be deployed. Even though Luke wasn't going to be in this rotation, he was still required to attend.

She found her father with a big pad of paper and a pencil, making some drawings. Her mother was outside with the girls, picking flowers and planting a flat of small chrysanthemums they had bought at the nursery the day before.

"You want some coffee, Dad?"

"Sure. Julie, I'd love some."

She set the mug on a coaster next to where he was drawing, and she peered over his shoulder.

"What are you doing?"

"I'm just sketching a few ideas I had."

"You're designing a new house?"

"I'm designing an addition."

"It looks huge. Is this something in Santa Rosa?"

Mr. Christensen put his pencil down and stared back at her. "Julie, I've been talking to your neighbor next door, and he's offered to sell me his property. I wanted to first talk to you before we actually execute something, but your mom and I have been thinking about something ever since the girls moved down here. With both of you working, we thought maybe we could help out, and living in Santa Rosa without Colin and Stephanie is just not what it used to be. We're constantly seeing things we did together as a family that we don't do anymore. It's actually been painful to be there all alone with all of you down here. So if you're okay with it—and please tell us if you're not, because we don't want to impose ourselves on you guys—we'd like to pursue purchasing the property and then perhaps design an addition for the house next door that would attach to this house. Or not. Whatever you choose. But if we combined the lots, we could do it and have room for everyone and have it look fabulous—a real oasis."

"You could actually swing that? Because our financial situation…"

"If we sell our property, we can pay cash for it. So we wouldn't have to ask your lender for approval. But we don't want to do that if you feel pressured in any way. It's just an idea."

Julie was amazed that he had come up with this and managed to keep it a secret from her.

"Does Luke know about this?"

He shook his head, "No."

"And you'd sell your house?" she asked.

"I've already had your realtor come over and give us an opinion of value. We own it free and clear, so we might be able to even carry paper and live off of the note proceeds. I think I'm done with that house. It did what it was designed to do. It was a nice place to raise you and Colin. But there comes a time when everything is behind and nothing is forward. I'd like something to look forward to. No matter what it is, Julie. Maybe we can't take care of the kids full time, but we could lend a hand. And it would perhaps save you having to hire somebody to come in on a regular basis to do that if you're both working. Your mom and I would like to do that. We really would."

"I'm delighted, Dad. I'd never even thought you'd consider something like that. The girls would be ecstatic."

"Good, and by the way, your realtor said to give her a call."

"What?"

"I think your phone's not charged, Julie. She's been trying to reach you since yesterday. You have an offer on the house. She said to tell you it's a really good offer, and you should give her a call."

CHAPTER 17

"**I**S THIS LUKE Paulsen?"

Luke was washing the van. Julie was inside, talking to her parents, enjoying her forced time off.

"Who is this?" He made a habit of never talking to someone unless he knew who they were. The fact that they called him on his personal, unlisted cell didn't make it any better.

"My name is Justin Hamblin. I believe you will recognize the name. I got your number from your trust attorney."

Luke wished he had a listening device he could click on, like when he was on special ops. He felt naked without his equipment.

"Luke?"

"Go on. What the hell do you want?"

"I have a proposition for you."

Figures.

"I'm not in the mood, Mr. Hamblin. You've done

some very damaging things to our family's reputation. My understanding is that you may be wanted by the law."

"Not aware of that, but I'm not surprised."

The guy sounded perfectly calm, and that pissed Luke off.

"I understand you're having some issues with the law as well, Mr. Paulsen. Maybe I can help."

"I doubt that."

"Just hear me out. I think I can help all this go away."

"You good at raising the dead too?"

"That was most unfortunate. That never should have happened."

"Damn right. They were murdered. Something tells me you were behind that."

"No, that wasn't me. Someone else made a huge miscalculation."

"Fuck you, you motherfucker!" Luke screamed into the phone. Then he searched the quiet Coronado neighborhood they lived in to see if anyone noticed. He didn't see any curtains being shut, cars stopping, or dogwalkers stopping in the street. He hoped no one had noticed. He didn't need that right now.

"If you will calm down, I have a solution to this never-ending saga that's befallen your family. I don't admit responsibility, Mr. Paulsen, if this call is being recorded. But I'm going to give you the opportunity to meet with my colleague to discuss arrangements that can make some or all of this go away."

"I think we're past that. If it's a fight you want, you've got it. And for the record, you are responsible for the leaks. I've had that verified by someone who knows, and I do hold you responsible for my baby sister's and my brother-in-law's deaths. I can't be talked down from that assumption, nor will I be talked down from spending the rest of my life seeing to it that you pay for it. I don't care how long it takes."

"At what cost, Mr. Paulsen?"

"Excuse me?"

"What cost would be too dear to pay? Aren't you concerned about the health and safety of your family? Do I have to give you their names and ages?"

Luke knew he should have thrown the phone in the gutter drain and called Riverton or Mayfield, but he didn't. It was the last thing he knew how to do, protect his family. It was too late for Steph and Colin.

"You better not—"

"I'm not talking about anything I would do, Mr. Paulsen. I know certain people who require certain documents to be returned to them. Until then, no one, even you, no one is safe, Mr. Paulsen."

He counted to ten. He envisioned cutting this man up, peeling the flesh from his skin, pulling every single tooth from his fucking skull, maybe removing his fingers joint by joint. He'd never done any of those things. Only animals did those things to people. But today, on this bright, sunny Coronado day, today, he could relish becoming that kind of a man, knowing full well there would be no coming back from that.

His revenge was much larger than his control.

LUKE TOLD JULIE he had to pick up a few things for the van. She started to show him the drawings her dad had made. He pretended he was capable of actually looking them over, envisioning a life with all of them together, seeing the girls living with their grandparents and all together, welcoming a new baby in the house, even if he needed to do diaper duty.

But he couldn't. His brittle smile was wide and sexy enough, taking a huge amount of effort to get there, that it fooled Julie.

He knew he should call Kyle. He should call someone else from the team, but that would get them into deep shit, even though they always said they had each other's back. That didn't mean following each other into the pits of hell. No, it didn't apply in that case.

Not telling them was a huge violation of the code of their brotherhood, but it was the only way he could keep them safe. Instead, he called Kyle and told him he had to run up to Santa Rosa to pick up something he'd left in the move. And he'd ask his LPO if he could have someone check in on Julie and the kids, just casually. Let them know he'd be back the next day.

"Why casually? Don't they know you're going or how long you'll be gone?"

"Not exactly."

"Fuck me, Luke. What have you done?"

"Nothing. I'm just going to go pick up something."

"Who are you going with?"

"No one. I don't need anyone to go up with me. I'm fine, Kyle. I was just asking for your eyes and ears for the family. Didn't want to spook them, you know, with all the shit going on?"

"Why not Mayfield or Riverton? They could do that."

"They're busy. And—"

"They're old. You need a fighter to protect them. Listen, Luke, you're about to do something you don't want to tell me about. I can tell when you're lying. You can't go do this on your own. Either I go with you, or you take someone from the team I pick out."

Luke thought about it. Should he take a shooter, an explosives guy, a medic, or—?

"Can I take Danny Begay? How about him?"

"The sling-shot guy."

"He's a shooter, you know that. He's been a help to me and knows the place I have to go to pick up this item. And he's calm."

"And you sure as hell aren't. Still not going to tell me?"

"Nothing to tell."

"Not yet, you mean. Okay, I'm going to call him and give him my advice. I'll leave it up to him whether or not he comes. You better not get the two of you tossed or, worse, wind up in jail. I can't afford to lose you guys."

And I can't afford to lose my family.

Ten minutes later, as Luke was picking up some things from the hardware store, Danny called him and asked that Luke pick him up outside the Skupper.

"I'm not going to share a beer with you, Danny. Either you're coming or you're not."

"Oh, I'm coming. I'm here with a couple of new recruits who didn't pass BUD/S. And they're getting drunk. I'm not. Me and Coop are babysitting. I'll let Coop do the rest. I'm going with you."

"Good deal."

"Just a clarification, do I need to bring my duty bag?"

"You probably should."

DANNY'S GEAR WAS in the secret compartment under the driver seat of his truck. He grabbed it, tossing it to Luke with a sneer.

"Don't make me regret this," he mumbled.

"I'm only asking for your protection. This isn't an action, and it sure as hell isn't an op. I have to meet with someone I don't trust."

Danny climbed into Luke's Hummer, and they sped toward the freeway north.

"Why not alert the locals? There are others who do this, you know."

"I can't. That's all I'm going to say."

"So who is this person?"

"I'm to meet with someone who wants something that was stored in a storage facility we didn't check. I got the key from Julie."

"So she's okay with this."

"She knows about it, yes." Luke hated lying to Danny, but it had to be that way. He'd find a way to make it up to him. But Kyle didn't leave him any room. He was going to blow up everything. And maybe he should, Luke pondered.

"What are we looking for then? Who is coming to get it?"

"I'm not sure who. But there's a bag stored in the back of Colin's Thunderbird. You remember that turquoise and white convertible he bought when he was down here? I didn't realize he still owned it. I don't know what's in the bag, but it could be papers for the car someone wants. I don't care a shit about that. I want to get these people off my back."

"These the people who have been telling stuff to the press and calling Kyle?"

"I think so."

"Fuck," Danny said as he peered out the windshield. "This have to do with that Feathers and Tails shit in Vegas?"

"Maybe."

"Maybe as in you don't know, or maybe yes, Luke?"

"I don't know. I've been promised that the issues we're facing are due to the fact that they need something back. They've been pressuring us. They don't really care about us. They just want us to do something. If I can solve this without any violence, without any more violence to my family, I think that's a good use of my time. Don't you?"

"So you're not going up there to off the guy, then?"

"That's not the plan. Ball's in his court." He abruptly pulled over at a rest stop. "I gotta pee. But let me tell you this, Danny, you are not to do anything except help keep me safe. No one is going to shoot or kill anyone, especially not you. Do you understand? I don't care what happens. If you can't save me, you walk away, and let destiny take its course. You do not risk your career. And I'm only bringing you because Kyle said I had to."

"I know about that. He's gonna want to know."

"He'll know soon enough. Don't tell him until he's too far away to be able to do anything. Okay, now I really gotta pee. You coming or staying here?"

"I'm staying with the shit. I'll go after you return."

IT TOOK ROUGHLY eight hours for the trip. Luke was pressing past the speed limit and was actively searching the horizon for little black-and-white friendlies. Danny helped with the lookouts.

He'd brought a ring of keys with him and, driving down Santa Rosa Avenue, stopped at a gated and attended mini-warehouse complex. He stopped into the office and inquired about the space Colin had rented, holding up the keys. He'd showed the young man a copy of the trust that stated he and Julie had the right to access it. It even had been listed in the trust.

The clerk searched through the ring, picked out the key with the unit number stamped on it, and handed it back to Luke.

"Is there anyone else here, asking for me?"

"No. Haven't seen anyone. We got people using their units today, but no one looking for you, not that I know of."

"Okay, we're going to drive down there. You see anyone who shouldn't be here, you call the cops first. You hear anything that sounds like a scuffle, you call the cops, okay?"

"Like they'd get here in the next four hours. But sure, I'll do that. Look, is there some kind of problem here? Is all this legit? I don't want to get into any trouble."

"No, sir. I'm a Navy SEAL. I've just lost my sister and brother-in-law, and I'm here to retrieve something that's important to the family. I'm just trying to be careful, is all."

"So if someone asks for you, I let them in?"

"Yessir. I'll be ready."

The facility consisted of rear units with tall doors large enough to store a regular RV. Then there were four rows of twelve-by-twelve storage units, all with roll-up metal doors. Colin's was at the end of one of the middle rows.

While Danny got out and walked around to the other side of the truck, watching the driveway from both directions, Luke opened the rollup door.

Colin's beautiful turquoise T-Bird sat all by itself. It was dusty, and all the tires were flat, indicating he hadn't been to the facility to work on it or take it for a stroll. He searched the key ring and found the distinctive key. He wanted to fire the thing up, but wasn't sure it was operable.

He looked up at Danny.

"We got company."

Luke walked outside to stand next to his teammate.

An old four-door pickup drove slowly toward them, a single driver, a young man with a baseball cap. He looked like a high school kid, scruffy and a bit dirty, like his truck, but otherwise not threatening. All his windows were rolled down, Luke noted.

The boy stopped about twenty feet away, sticking his head out of the window frame.

"You Luke?"

"Yessir. Who are you?"

"I'm Justin Hamblin."

He didn't sound anything like the person Luke had talked to on the phone.

"No, you're not." Luke walked over towards the driver door, and the boy demanded he stop. Out of the side of his eye, he saw Danny assuming a shooting stance, without producing a weapon.

"I said stop!" the boy yelled.

"You packing, Son? You got a gun you gonna use?" Luke demanded. "It'd be two against one, and I already told the clerk up front to call the cops."

Someone rose up from the second seat, shoving a long gun in his face, but he growled in Jason Hamblin's voice, "No, it's be two against two. Don't be stupid, Luke. That kid never got that call off."

If Hamblin lowered the weapon or Luke saw something from the boy, he was going to grab the Sig Sauer tucked into his back. But he'd have to move quick and shoot whatever moved. He didn't want to do that. Not yet.

He flicked his fingers, preparing himself for what he hoped he didn't have to do, and giving Danny a clue that he was ready, but he didn't encourage his buddy.

Just then, from each side, two vehicles drove in, with screeching tires and a cloud of dust and gravel scattering everywhere. One landed behind the old truck, the other on the other side of Luke's Hummer, effectively closing any of them from an easy escape.

Hamblin swung his weapon around to the back and took aim at the cloud of dust, but he was shot in the arm, forcing him to drop the AR-15 rifle he'd been holding.

He heard a familiar voice before the kid scrambled out of the front seat and ran past Luke and Danny. He ended up in the arms of three fully locked and loaded Navy SEALs who had driven behind them.

"You dumb motherfucker! I told you not to get involved in this shit. Now look at what you made—who fired on this poor gentleman?" Kyle Lansdowne barked.

Nobody answered.

Hamblin was writhing in pain on the ground, but he was trying to crawl slowly away until Coop came up to him and stepped on his arm, where the wound was, which made the man have an early conversion and pee his pants.

"This guy's all fucked up," Coop said. "Someone help this guy up while I get my kit."

Luke was frozen in place.

"Get rid of the guns, dumbass," Kyle said. "Put 'em away. The cops are on their way."

Both Danny and Luke did so, just as two Santa Rosa police cruisers came barreling down the alleyway with their sirens blaring.

"Thought you didn't want to get involved."

"No, you didn't want to get us involved, Luke, remember? Besides, we aren't involved. We came by just to make sure you were okay, with all this crap going on. I think this guy's buddy shot him by mistake."

"Kyle, you're a fuckin' liar."

"I'm a better liar than you are."

"Thanks, Man."

"I told you not to do this alone. You can't do anything alone. Not when you're on my team, Son. We're putting you on a plane tonight, Luke. Now you have to do something even harder. You're going to have to make up with your wife. She's not very happy, Luke. Not happy at all. You might have fixed this, but I'm not sure you can fix that."

CHAPTER 18

JULIE HAD TAKEN the news of Luke's trip with fury at first, then alarm, and then found herself drowning with a huge foreboding she couldn't shake. Her mother had her go to bed, rest, and wait, especially for the sake of the baby. Kyle had called her, letting her know what Luke was doing and why, and promised he'd update her. He told her not to doubt the team was going to do everything they could to bring Luke back safely.

But Luke's decision to take off had her worried he might have landed in some dark place he wouldn't be able to dig his way out of.

He'd worked so hard. They all had. How could he betray their trust, leave without saying goodbye? She was his partner, yet he called Kyle, his LPO, not her!

Was she married to a man or a team? Was this going to be their new life if he stayed with SEAL Team 3? Would she always have to worry forever that whenever he left for the store he'd never return? How selfish and unfeeling this was. Didn't he care anything about her or the kids?

Or was he going off to end everything? Had the stress of these past few weeks just welled up so much that he had to take himself out in a blaze of glory. Julie thought he'd been doing so well, seemed to be happy with the new baby on the way, accepted the idea that her parents were going to live next to them. What set him off and what made him decide it was a good idea to not include her in this drastic decision?

Luci Begay came over later on and stayed for a bit, trying to console her. She was told others would be coming. While being thankful, Julie wanted to hear from Luke. He was her whole world. And why couldn't he understand that?

Luci tried to help her with answers.

"I couldn't talk Danny down. But he discussed it with Kyle, and he felt, we all felt Luke needed backup to come home safely to you and his family. Many of his buds on the team didn't trust the local law enforcement officers, didn't have a relationship with them like they did here, so it was not a problem signing up for this mission, Julie. It was to save Luke's life."

"But why couldn't he tell me?"

"Maybe he didn't know what to say. Maybe he just knew nothing you could say would change his mind and he wanted to just go for it? Doesn't make it right, but I've heard about things like this happening. Julie, they never listen. You know they don't. They march to a different drummer. We have to trust that they're doing the right thing. But we never can control it. You know that."

Julie did realize Luke didn't do it for the excitement of doing something against the people they held responsible for Colin and Steph's death or the crap coming at the family right now. He did it for them, not for him. Either way, there was no satisfaction for him. Either way, he violated some trust.

And he chose to violate the trust between the two of them.

Why?

At dusk, when she hadn't heard anything, she tried to call Luke's cell and got no answer. Then she tried Kyle's cell, and the same thing happened.

And then she got the call she'd been waiting for all day.

"Hi, Babe."

"Luke! Oh my God! Are you okay?" Her steely resolve melted at the sound of his voice. Then the wave of fear she'd been holding onto splashed over her. "You know I'm angry at you. You violated your oath to me, your promise. How can I ever trust you again?"

"I'm so sorry. I will understand if you can't take me

back. I felt I had no choice. Jules, I wouldn't be able to live with myself if I didn't get this guy out of our lives."

"What? Did you kill him?"

"No, I didn't kill him. I didn't even shoot him. He got shot by someone else. But he's locked up, and hopefully, he'll be put away for a long time for endangering all of us and for causing the accident that took Colin and Stephanie's life."

"What was this about?"

"It's a long story. Right now, I'm just about to go into a briefing. I got Kyle, Danny, Coop, T.J., Tucker, and other guys too. We all have to be questioned by the police. But I'll sit down with you and explain everything. I promise. I'm so sorry. It's the last time I'll ever do anything like this again."

She wanted to believe him, but she had to be realistic, as well. If she didn't face the facts, she'd always be wondering, and she'd always be a mess. The kids deserved to have a mother who was present, looked after them, and kept them healthy and safe. Not someone filled with rage and resentment.

"When are you returning to us?"

"As soon as this is over. Tonight. They're going to put me on a plane tonight. The rest of the guys are driving home, bringing back my truck."

"Where did you go? Where in Santa Rosa? To the house—which, by the way, is sold."

"That's good news. I was at the storage facility that housed Colin's Thunderbird. He'd stored some incriminating evidence in the trunk, and the guy needed it back. I also think he had designs to off me, as well, to solve another issue. The guys saved my life, honey. I would have done and will do the same for them."

Of all the things Luke told her, the last sentence was the honest truth.

"Soon, Sweetheart. And if I'm lucky enough to earn a second chance with you, I promise you won't regret it. I'll be a model husband, Julie. I'll do anything you want whenever you want it."

She was beginning to get ideas already.

It was one o'clock in the morning when he returned to their bedroom. A taxi had picked him up from the airport. He walked in without his bags, which he left in the Hummer with Danny and the guys, and collapsed in her arms.

"I'm so sorry, Julie," he sobbed.

She found her heart needing to show him the tenderness and love she had for him. Her big, fucked up, tatted mess of a man, this self-proclaimed "killing machine with a heart the size of the ocean."

One thing she knew as sure as the fact that she was alive, Luke needed her. And he wasn't afraid to show it, either. It had not always been this way, especially in the beginning when they were first getting together. But without her, she was certain he'd be lost.

But as she held him, listened to his sobs, felt how he clutched her nightgown and clung to her like a little child, she realized she needed him just as much.

She stroked his head, kissed his forehead, then begged him to strip down and just come to bed. She wanted to soothe all his rough parts, cover the scars, and kiss and love away all the deficiencies. He was a complicated package, a man who hadn't started out strong like some of the other teammates, but who had fought for his own sanity, for his family, for his career probably harder than anyone else she'd met.

He wasn't perfect. But he was all hers. And every inch of her belonged to Luke and always would.

He was home.

EPILOGUE

JUSTIN HAMBLIN WASN'T his real name, which wasn't a surprise to anybody. He'd been a recruiter for picking up young girls to bring them into the trade as sex workers. It had started when he began running illegals across the border. Earned a lot of money doing it, and he looked for investments he could make with his new-found fortune.

He'd run across the Garden of Delights mail order business quite by accident. He was invited to a party by a raunchy hostess who was training young girls to pleasure their Johns better. He saw a way to legitimize his business.

Stephanie seemed like the perfect mark, until he discovered her brother was a Navy SEAL, and he almost quit right there. But he'd spent time recruiting her to the party scheme, without her ever knowing what he was really doing. And when she needed help with her successful business, he was only too pleased to introduce her to one of his recruits, who had actually aspired to become an office manager one day with her knowledge of computers. A runaway who needed a mother and would do anything for money.

When Colin and Stephanie weren't looking too closely, he managed to sell devices to other trailer camps and ranches with the help of his recruit.

And then his girl fell in love. It was the bane of any pimp. She fell in love with one of her regulars she was working on the side, and he took her away.

Under the guise that she was in trouble and needed money, she got Stephanie to empty her bank account. But not before she delivered a package of photographs he'd been storing. Disgusting child porn, videos of mostly immigrant kids being abused.

Of course, they wanted out. Colin insisted they terminate their relationship and held the photos over him. So it has been time to scare Steph and Colin, scare them into giving up everything, including the incriminating evidence, so they could never again be a thorn in his side.

Except his helper didn't do what he'd been asked. He'd used a semi cab instead of the truck he was supposed to use and killed them both.

It really was an accident.

Had he got the photos, it would have been fine. He already had most the money and was expecting more.

Colin had offered to take a mortgage out on the house and had started the process, and with all that money, he would have been set. He could retire to Mexico or Central America until things cooled off. And then he'd start anew. It would have been a fresh start. He would have learned from his mistakes of the past and looked forward to a lucrative future.

But this damned family—the Navy SEAL asshole who went off like a bull in a China shop, his doggedly stubborn marks who wouldn't give up no matter what he threatened, and the young recruit whose life was transformed by love, all these things worked against him.

And he failed.

But when he got out, he'd be back. He'd find someone else to latch onto and milk for their assets. There were always people trying to come to the U.S. for a better life. There were millions of people out there he could use and abuse.

And he could wait. Besides, they'd decriminalized prostitution in most parts of California. Nevada had legalized it. Nobody was watching the border, and everyone wanted to party and have a good time.

All except these damned Navy SEAL families. He wouldn't make that mistake again.

Did you enjoy Destiny of Love, Book 6 in the SEAL Brotherhood: Legacy series? Are you ready for Book 7, Heart of Gold, which you can preorder here?

And if you want to read more about Destiny of Love's main characters, Luke and Julie, like how they met, got started, and fell in love, be sure to read SEAL My Destiny, which is Book 6 of the original SEAL Brotherhood series and takes place ten years before Destiny of Love.

Here are the SEAL series more or less in order for your reading enjoyment:

SEAL Brotherhood

SEAL Brotherhood: Legacy

Bad Boys of SEAL Team 3

Band of Bachelors

Bone Frog Brotherhood

Bone Frog Bachelor

Sunset SEALs

Shadow SEALs

And have you met Sharon's new pen name Annie Carr?

ABOUT THE AUTHOR

NYT and USA/Today Bestselling Author Sharon Hamilton's SEAL Brotherhood series have earned her author rankings of #1 in Romantic Suspense, Military Romance and Contemporary Romance. Her other *Brotherhood* stand-alone series are: Bad Boys of SEAL Team 3, Band of Bachelors, True Blue SEALs, Nashville SEALs, Bone Frog Brotherhood, Sunset SEALs, Bone Frog Bachelor Series and SEAL Brotherhood Legacy Series. She is a contributing author to the very popular Shadow SEALs multi-author series.

Her SEALs and former SEALs have invested in two wineries, a lavender farm and a brewery in Sonoma County, which have become part of the new stories. They also have expanded to include Veteran-benefit projects on the Florida Gulf Coast, as well as projects in Africa and the Maldives. One of the SEAL wives has even launched her own women's fiction series. But old characters, as well as children of these SEAL heroes keep returning to all the newer books.

Sharon also writes sexy paranormals in two series: Golden Vampires of Tuscany and The Guardians.

A lifelong organic vegetable and flower gardener, Sharon and her husband lived for fifty years in the Wine Country of Northern California, where many of her stories take place. Recently, they have moved to the beautiful Gulf Coast of Florida, with stories of shipwrecks, the white sugar-sand beaches of Sunset, Treasure Island and Indian Rocks Beaches.

She loves hearing from fans through her website: authorsharonhamilton.com

Find out more about Sharon, her upcoming releases, appearances and news when you sign up for Sharon's newsletter.

Facebook:
facebook.com/SharonHamiltonAuthor

Twitter:
twitter.com/sharonlhamilton

Pinterest:
pinterest.com/AuthorSharonH

Amazon:
amazon.com/Sharon-Hamilton/e/B004FQQMAC

BookBub:
bookbub.com/authors/sharon-hamilton

Youtube:

youtube.com/channel/UCDInkxXFpXp_4Vnq08ZxMBQ

Soundcloud:

soundcloud.com/sharon-hamilton-1

Sharon Hamilton's Rockin' Romance Readers:

facebook.com/groups/sealteamromance

Sharon Hamilton's Goodreads Group:

goodreads.com/group/show/199125-sharon-hamilton-readers-group

Visit Sharon's Online Store:

sharon-hamilton-author.myshopify.com

Join Sharon's Review Teams:

eBook Reviews:

sharonhamiltonassistant@gmail.com

Audio Reviews:

sharonhamiltonassistant@gmail.com

Life is one fool thing after another.
Love is two fool things after each other.

REVIEWS

PRAISE FOR THE
GOLDEN VAMPIRES OF TUSCANY SERIES

"Well to say the least I was thoroughly surprise. I have read many Vampire books, from Ann Rice to Kym Grosso and few other Authors, so yes I do like Vampires, not the super scary ones from the old days, but the new ones are far more interesting far more human than one can remember. I found Honeymoon Bite a totally engrossing book, I was not able to put it down, page after page I found delight, love, understanding, well that is until the bad bad Vamp started being really bad. But seeing someone love another person so much that they would do anything to protect them, well that had me going, then well there was more and for a while I thought it was the end of a beautiful love story that spanned not only time but, spanned Italy and California. Won't divulge how it ended, but I did shed a few tears after screaming but Sharon Hamilton did not let me down, she took me on amazing trip that I loved, look forward to reading another Vampire book of hers."

"An excellent paranormal romance that was exciting, romantic, entertaining and very satisfying to read. It had me anticipating what would happen next many times over, so much so I could not put it down and even finished it up in a day. The vampires in this book were different from your average vampire, but I enjoy different variations and changes to the same old stuff. It made for a more unpredictable read and more adventurous to explore! Vampire lovers, any paranormal readers and even those who love the romance genre will enjoy Honeymoon Bite."

"This is the first non-Seal book of this author's I have read and I loved it. There is a cast-like hierarchy in this vampire community with humans at the very bottom and Golden vampires at the top. Lionel is a dark vampire who are servants of the Goldens. Phoebe is a Golden who has not decided if she will remain human or accept the turning to become a vampire. Either way she and Lionel can never be together since it is forbidden.

I enjoyed this story and I am looking forward to the next installment."

"A hauntingly romantic read. Old love lost and new love found. Family, heart, intrigue and vampires. Grabbed my attention and couldn't put down. Would definitely recommend."

PRAISE FOR THE
SEAL BROTHERHOOD SERIES

"Fans of Navy SEAL romance, I found a new author to feed your addiction. Finely written and loaded delicious with moments, Sharon Hamilton's storytelling satisfies like a thick bar of chocolate." —Marliss Melton, bestselling author of the *Team Twelve* Navy SEALs series

"Sharon Hamilton does an EXCELLENT job of fitting all the characters into a brotherhood of SEALS that may not be real but sure makes you feel that you have entered the circle and security of their world. The stories intertwine with each book before...and each book after and THAT is what makes Sharon Hamilton's SEAL Brotherhood Series so very interesting. You won't want to put down ANY of her books and they will keep you reading into the night when you should be sleeping. Start with this book...and you will not want to stop until you've read the whole series and then...you will be waiting for Sharon to write the next one." (5 Star Review)

"Kyle and Christy explode all over the pages in this first book, *[Accidental SEAL]*, in a whole new series of SEALs. If the twist and turns don't get your heart jumping, then maybe the suspense will. This is a must read for those that are looking for love and adventure with a little sloppy love thrown in for good measure." (5 Star Review)

PRAISE FOR THE
BAD BOYS OF SEAL TEAM 3 SERIES

"I love reading this series! Once you start these books, you can hardly put them down. The mix of romance and suspense keeps you turning the pages one right after another! Can't wait until the next book!" (5 Star Review)

"I love all of Sharon's Seal books, but *[SEAL's Code]* may just be her best to date. Danny and Luci's journey is filled with a wonderful insight into the Native American life. It is a love story that will fill you with warmth and contentment. You will enjoy Danny's journey to become a SEAL and his reasons for it. Good job Sharon!" (5 Star Review)

PRAISE FOR THE
BAND OF BACHELORS SERIES

"*[Lucas]* was the first book in the Band of Bachelors series and it was a phenomenal start. I loved how we got to see the other SEALs we all love and we got a look at Lucas and Marcy. They had an instant attraction, and their love was very intense. This book had it all, suspense, steamy romance, humor, everything you want in a riveting, outstanding read. I can't wait to read the next book in this series." (5 Star Review)

PRAISE FOR THE
TRUE BLUE SEALS SERIES

"Keep the tissues box nearby as you read *True Blue SEALs: Zak* by Sharon Hamilton. I imagine more than I wish to that the circumstances surrounding Zak and Amy are all too real for returning military personnel and their families. Ms. Hamilton has put us right in the middle of struggles and successes that these two high school sweethearts endure. I have read several of Sharon Hamilton's military romances but will say this is the most emotionally intense of the ones that I have read. This is a well-written, realistic story with authentic characters that will have you rooting for them and proud of those who serve to keep us safe. This is an author who writes amazing stories that you love and cry with the characters. Fans of Jessica Scott and Marliss Melton will want to add Sharon Hamilton to their list of realistic military romance writers." (5 Star Review)

"Dear FATHER IN HEAVEN,

If I may respectfully say so sometimes you are a strange God. Though you love all mankind,

It seems you have special predilections too.

You seem to love those men who can stand up alone who face impossible odds, Who challenge every bully and every tyrant ~

Those men who know the heat and loneliness of Calvary. Possibly you cherish men of this stamp because you recognize the mark of your only son in them.

Since this unique group of men known as the SEALs know Calvary and suffering, teach them now the mystery of the resurrection ~ that they are indestructible, that they will live forever because of their deep faith in you.

And when they do come to heaven, may I respectfully warn you, Dear Father, they also know how to celebrate. So please be ready for them when they insert under your pearly gates.

Bless them, their devoted Families and their Country on this glorious occasion.

We ask this through the merits of your Son, Christ Jesus the Lord, Amen."

By Reverend E.J. McMalhon S.J. LCDR, CHC, USN
Awards Ceremony SEAL Team One
1975 At NAB, Coronado